The Wilde One

Janelle Denison

Print Edition
Cover Photo Copyright July 2014, Novel Graphic Designs
Formatting by BB eBooks

Chapter One

Adrian Wilde took a long swallow of his beer in honor of the three-day relaxing weekend stretching ahead of him and nearly choked on the drink when he caught sight of Chayse Douglas, the one woman he'd spent the past four months turning down and trying to avoid. Standing at the bar as she ordered a drink, she waggled her fingers at him in greeting and smiled in a way that made him feel like a hunted man.

You can run but you can't hide…

He all but heard the words conveyed in that determined look of hers, and his body warmed with a familiar lust he'd been fighting since the moment he'd met her, followed closely by annoyance. That she'd ventured into such a public place as Nick's Sports Bar to fight for her cause was enough to put him on full alert, and it didn't surprise him that she'd enlisted his hellion cousin, Mia Wilde, to help persuade him into agreeing to be a part of Chayse's beefcake calendar project.

He thought he'd finally convinced the pint-sized bundle of fortitude that he wasn't interested in posing half-naked for her Outdoor Men Calendar. Since he knew she had a deadline to meet, he'd assumed she'd found another willing victim and he was off the hook. But having been the recipient of that purposeful gleam in those violet-hued eyes, Adrian knew, without a single doubt, that the delectable Chayse still had her sights set on him.

Christ. While he admired her tenacity to go after what she wanted and found her brazen pursuit too much of a turn-on, she was setting herself up for another dose of rejection, because there was no way in hell he was going to change his mind. He was doing her a huge favor by saying no. While she might think he was exactly what she wanted for her calendar, he was far from model material.

Frustrated by the entire situation, along with his unwanted attraction to Chayse that made everything all the more complicated, he returned his attention to his table mates and eyed them suspiciously. "Who the hell tipped off Mia that we'd be here tonight?" he demanded, because that was the only way Chayse could have found him so easily.

Three pairs of curious eyes glanced toward the bar, where he'd pointed his bottle of beer. His brother Steve sat next to him on the left, then there was Cameron, Steve's good friend and business partner, and their cousin Scott, older brother to Mia.

Cameron, who'd been fighting his own battle of the sexes with Mia, shook his head adamantly. "Not me, man. The last thing I'd do is invite the wild child to crash our little party and ruin my perfectly good evening."

Adrian believed him, though the fire and challenge in Cameron's eyes spoke a tale of their own. Cameron wasn't altogether upset about Mia's appearance. Not that he'd ever admit to the attraction that sizzled to life whenever the two of them were in the same room.

Adrian's gaze shifted to Steve's, and his older brother held up his hands in defense. "Hey, I haven't spoken to Mia all week."

Which left Scott, and judging by the sheepish look on his cousin's face, Adrian rightly assumed the man was responsible for this interesting turn of events. "'Fess up, Scotty-boy," Adrian said.

Scott shrugged. "Okay, so I was leaving the office today and casually mentioned I was coming here for a drink with some friends. When Mia asked who with, I wasn't about to lie."

"Your honesty is a refreshing and noble trait," Adrian drawled wryly, giving his cousin a hard time. "Next time, *lie*."

Cameron and Steve chuckled in amusement.

Scott leaned back in his chair and absently stroked his finger along his jaw while regarding Adrian speculatively. "Why do I get the feeling that your problem isn't so much with Mia but that hot little number she's with?"

Adrian downed the rest of his beer and motioned to the bar waitress for another one, wondering if he ought to order a chaser to go with it. "Because she's the photographer who's been dogging me for the past four months to do that damn beefcake calendar for charity, and she's having one helluva time taking no for an answer."

His male counterparts offered nods of understanding and grunts of sympathy, and a moment later, Mia and Chayse were strolling across the establishment toward their table, each with one of those fancy, designer martini drinks in hand.

Despite himself, Adrian took in the long-sleeved, pink cotton shirt that clung to Chayse's petite curves and snug jeans that outlined the gentle flare of her hips and the rest of her compact body. He'd noticed more than once that she had small but firm breasts, maybe a handful by his experienced estimation, and that was being generous considering he had large palms and long fingers. Not that he'd ever get the opportunity to test the weight and size of those luscious mounds in his hands, except for in his dreams. Oh, yeah, in those nightly fantasies, he'd caressed those soft breasts of hers, and a whole lot more.

"Hello, boys," Mia said cheerfully. "Mind if we join you?"

"Yes," Adrian and Cameron echoed at the same

time Scott and Steve said graciously, "Not at all."

The women opted to ignore Adrian and Cameron and accepted Scott and Steve's invitation. Dragging two nearby chairs up to the table, Chayse flanked Adrian on one side with Mia on the other, which put Mia conveniently right next to Cameron. Mia, with her stylishly cut black hair and exotic silver eyes, slanted Cameron a smug grin full of her brand of sensual torment. He met her gaze unflinchingly, the instantaneous sparks of awareness between the two of them nearly tangible.

As was the feverish heat and undeniable hunger Chayse generated whenever she was near him, Adrian thought as the waitress delivered his second beer. He took a long drink of the cold brew, which did nothing to extinguish the fire that had started in his chest and was gradually spiraling its way lower.

Damn her, anyway.

Setting the bottle on the table, Adrian reclined in his chair, glanced at the woman sitting next to him, and met that direct, sultry gaze of hers that never failed to unnerve him. It wasn't so much the rare, extraordinary violet color that disturbed him but, rather, the way those eyes seemed to see past the footloose and fancy-free rules he'd lived by the past few years. Rules that kept his real emotions under wraps. Her pursuit felt personal, as if she found him much too intriguing to give up on. And quite frankly, her uncanny ability to unsettle him so effortlessly scared the crap out of him.

Thank God she had no clue how much she affected him. And she never would, he vowed, because he wasn't about to let down his guard or allow her to rattle his control.

Then she smiled. A slow, sensual smile that affected him like a blow right to the gut. Just that easily, just that quick, he ached to kiss those pink, glossy lips of hers, wanted to eat her up, inch by delectable inch and taste her in every hot, sweet, womanly place. Most of all, he wanted to push her up against the nearest wall and let her feel exactly what she did to him.

Shrugging off his too-stimulating thoughts, he lifted a brow her way. "What a coincidence meeting you here," he said and didn't bother tempering the edge of sarcasm in his tone.

She laughed off his scorn, the lilting sound full of confidence. "What can I say? I'm a determined woman. When I find something I want, I go after it until I've exhausted every possible approach."

And what she wanted was him. "More like obstinate and too damned tenacious," he muttered, though loud enough for her, and everyone else, to hear.

"I think her persistence is very admirable." Scott lifted his beer to Chayse in a mock salute.

"Why, thank you." Chayse beamed at Scott for his support. "Being persistent has definitely served me well."

Adrian narrowed his gaze and pointed a threatening finger at his cousin, who'd dared to take her side. "Nobody asked your opinion, Scotty, so I'd appreciate it if you kept it to yourself."

Chayse returned her attention to him, amusement dancing in her eyes. "If *you* weren't being so stubborn, I wouldn't have to be so persistent."

She ran her fingers though her permanently tousled, chin-length, honey-blonde curls, combing them away from her face, a habit of hers he found too damn fascinating and tempting. Most of the rebellious strands sprang back into place, and Adrian's fingers itched to push them back again, just as an excuse to see if her hair was as silky-soft as it looked.

He wrapped his hand tight around his bottle of beer and scowled at her. "Don't you have a deadline that's come and gone?"

"I got an extension." She took a sip of her green martini, and he caught the scent of apples just before she slowly licked her lips and his libido kicked into overdrive. "I have one more week, and I've decided that I'm going to make you my main priority and stalk you until you finally give in." Her tone was teasing, but her gaze told him just how serious her intentions were.

Well, he wasn't going to be around for her to stalk, thank God. For the next three days, he'd be at the family cabin catching up on some R and R and enjoying a weekend of peace and solitude.

"Don't count on me changing my mind, sweetheart," he told her. "My answer is, and will always remain, no thank you."

"Aww, come on Adrian," Mia piped in, disappointment lacing her voice. "This is for charity, for crying out loud. I can't believe you'd say no to something that would benefit so many kids at the Children's Hospital."

Adrian's jaw clenched tightly, but he remained quiet. Mia's comment made him sound cold and unfeeling, when his reasons for refusing had nothing to do with being selfish. Rather, he was self-conscious about baring so much of his less-than-perfect body to the thousands of people who purchased the calendar. But he wasn't about to reveal his personal, private reasons to Chayse, or anyone else, for that matter.

Cameron slanted Mia an incredulous glance. "Contrary to popular belief, not all men are into being displayed as sexual objects."

"Since when?" Mia argued and leaned closer to Cameron, clearly relishing a debate with him. "Come on, admit it, sugar. Being the object of a woman's fantasies is a nice stroke to the male ego."

He frowned at her, impatience and something more heated smoldering in Cameron's gold-flecked eyes. "I'll admit to nothing, except that you're a female chauvinist."

She propped her chin in her hand and batted her lashes at him, unfazed by his accusation. "I'm a liberated woman and proud of it."

Before Cameron could supply a comeback, Steve

steered the conversation in a different and unexpected direction. "What about Scott here, Chayse?" Steve clapped the other man on the back. "He's in great physical shape, he's not bad on the eyes, and he's single. Maybe you could convince him to take his clothes off for your cause."

Scott looked mortified at the thought. "Uh, I don't think so."

Chayse laughed and took another swallow of her martini. "Don't worry, Scott. While you'd make quite the eye candy for my calendar, you're off the hook," she reassured him, then shifted her unwavering gaze back to Adrian. She swirled the cherry that had accompanied her drink in the last bit of liquor, then popped the juicy piece of fruit into her mouth and chewed. "You, on the other hand, are just what I'm looking for to complete my Outdoor Men Calendar. Like the three other men who've posed for my project, you're the real thing. You're a sports enthusiast who takes it to the extreme, you own Wilde Adventures, which caters to outdoor recreational activities, and you epitomize everything an outdoor man should look like and be."

She scooted back her chair and stood, and for a moment, Adrian thought she was going to leave and experienced an inexplicable combination of relief and disappointment.

"I need to run to the ladies' room," she said instead and flashed him a quick, I'm-not-done-with-you-yet look. "Maybe while I'm gone, these guys and Mia can talk some sense into you."

With that bold statement, she sauntered away, hips swaying in those snug jeans of hers. He watched her stroll past the crowded dance floor to the corridor that led to the restrooms, then finally glanced back at his brother, Cameron, and his cousins, who were all eyeing him with varying degrees of interest, anticipation, and amusement.

Mia opened her mouth to speak, and Adrian cut her off with a wave of his hand. "Don't *even* go there."

Steve wasn't so easily intimidated. "I have to admit, she puts up a convincing argument."

"I'm not interested. Period. End of discussion." He polished off his beer and refrained from ordering a third.

"Fine." Steve's stare was all too knowing. "But just for the record, I think the little spitfire has gotten to you, and maybe this is possibly about more than just posing for a beefcake calendar."

Adrian's first instinct was to deny Steve's very astute statement. But his older brother knew him well, knew what he'd been through in the past, and knew the emotional wringer one woman had put him through that had affected his views on relationships with the female gender and had him not letting any woman close ever since.

Steve sighed and stood. "And on that note, I'm outta here. I promised Liz I'd help her close up The

Daily Grind tonight, and I'm hoping to get a caramel Frappuccino out of the deal." He waggled his brows, indicating that he was hoping for a whole lot more than just a cold coffee drink from his wife.

Scott grinned. "How's married life?"

Withdrawing a large bill from his wallet, Steve tossed it onto the table for his drink and tip. "A helluva lot better than this," he said and indicated the single scene behind him gathered at Nick's to enjoy the band, play pool or darts, and generally attempt to pick up members of the opposite sex.

Cameron shook his head and rocked his chair onto the back legs. "You and Eric are something else, from sworn bachelors to domestic bliss. You're making us look bad."

"What can I say, boys? I'm living the good life." The broad smile on Steve's face attested to just how happy he was. "When the right woman comes along, then you'll understand the domestic bliss thing and actually enjoy it."

With a round of good-nights, Steve left the bar, leaving Adrian to contemplate his brother's comment and how the right woman had changed both Steve's and Eric's bachelor lives. He'd never seen either of his brothers so mellow before, so content in their lives and the women they'd married. Adrian was beginning to feel like the odd man out lately, and restless in a way he couldn't shake. Which was why he'd decided to escape for the weekend to the family cabin—a quiet sanctuary away from work and the craziness of life. Not to mention the old, painful memories that had been nagging him ever since Chayse had made him a target for her pinup calendar and he'd realized he wanted her in ways that defied the keep-it-simple rules he'd set for himself four years ago.

Undoubtedly, he was an earthy, physical guy who loved sex and all the pleasures to be found in a woman's body, and he could always find a warm and eager female when the mood struck him. But that was all he allowed anymore … just hot, mindless sex with women who knew the score right up front and wanted the same thing. To that end, he didn't care what they thought of him or how he looked in their eyes, because it was all about mutual give-and-take and carnal satisfaction, and they both walked away afterward with no expectations or regrets.

He scrubbed a hand along his jaw, forced to admit that even raucous sex with a ready and willing partner had lost its appeal over the past few months. And he had a certain stubborn, persistent blonde-haired beauty to blame for his lack of interest in any other woman, and his celibate life of late.

Chayse was so under his skin, and he couldn't get her out of his mind, his erotic dreams, his life, no matter how hard he tried. And whenever he felt the vibes between them, which was anytime they were in the same vicinity, it nearly devastated his senses and destroyed his restraint. Yet beyond their sexual attraction, she exuded warmth and a genuine caring he was inexplicably drawn to, especially when she talked about her project or the kids at Chicago's Children's Hospital, where she visited and was a volunteer.

He cast an irritable glance toward the restrooms just as Chayse exited. She headed back in the direction of the table, only to be waylaid by a tall, good-looking guy who grasped her elbow. She stopped, surprised but not upset by the man's interception. He motioned to the dance floor with a charming smile and a nod of his head. She shrugged her shoulders in a sure-why-not kind of gesture, and off they went together, mingling into the crowd dancing to the rock music the band was playing.

The pair started out innocently enough, with Chayse seemingly enjoying herself, but it didn't take long for Casanova to make a move, using their close proximity to initiate a little touchy-feely with her. His hands came to rest on her shimmying hips, then boldly slipped around to her backside.

Jealousy, a sensation Adrian hadn't experienced in much too long, reared its ugly head before he could stop the emotion. His temper flared at the other man's predatory move toward Chayse, a possessive, unwelcome response he *refused* to act upon.

"Jesus, Adrian," Scott said, cutting through his dark, festering thoughts. "Would you stop glaring already?"

"That guy has his hand on her ass," he bit out,

disgusted with himself for caring so much.

Cameron grinned with keen male insight. "And you wish it was *your* hand on her ass instead, don't you?"

Adrian couldn't argue the truth, so he didn't even try. Through a narrowed gaze, he watched as Chayse removed the other man's wandering hands from her bottom, but the chump merely grabbed her around the waist, jerked her hips to his, and ground himself lewdly against her. She stiffened and braced her hands against his shoulders to hold him away, but her partner wasn't letting go and used the crush of people around them to his advantage.

Adrian's hand curled into a fist, and the muscles in his arm bunched with tension. He wanted to pummel the guy, then tear him apart, limb by limb. "He's practically molesting her out on the dance floor."

"Then maybe you ought to go over there and do something about it," Mia suggested oh-so-helpfully.

"Maybe I will." Watching the other man ignore Chayse's attempt to slip from his grasp again, Adrian felt as though he'd been prodded with a hot brand, provoked beyond reason. Because it certainly wasn't any sort of reasoning that had him strolling across the bar room and into the fray of writhing, dancing bodies to rescue her.

Coming up behind the guy, Adrian placed his hand where neck met shoulder and applied a firm pressure with his fingers that immediately caught the other man's attention.

"What the hell?" The other man instantly let go of Chayse and tried to whirl around to face his accoster, but Adrian's unrelenting hold prevented him from moving freely.

"The lady's with me," Adrian said, low and menacing, and gave the guy a push to the side. "Touch her again and I won't be responsible for my actions."

The other man straightened his shirt and shot Adrian a scathing glance. But after taking one look at Adrian's superior size and strength, the chump obviously thought better of challenging him and left the dance floor.

Adrian had every intention of dragging Chayse back to the table, but before he could do so, she slipped her hands around his neck, ensnaring him with her arms and holding him in place with her sultry, disarming gaze.

She shook her head in wonder, causing those soft, disheveled waves to caress her cheek and jaw. "Talk about trading one bundle of trouble for another," she teased.

"Just say thank you," he said gruffly and placed his hands lightly on her slender waist because it was the safest place to keep them when he was so damned tempted to slide them elsewhere.

She swayed closer with the beat of the music, aligning their bodies even more intimately than she'd been with the previous guy. This time, of her own free will. "Thank you, though I didn't need the help."

His body responded to the warmth and softness of her supple curves, hardening him in a scalding rush of need. "What? You like being mauled by men?"

She laughed, the provocative vibration causing her breasts to jiggle enticingly against his chest. "Now that all depends on the man and the situation, though I have to agree that he wasn't the right man *or* situation. If you hadn't shown up when you did, he would have been the very unhappy recipient of my knee jamming up against his groin."

He winced at that unpleasant image and quickly realized that this sassy, spirited woman could have easily held her own with her dance partner.

"You, however, are the right man, in *many* ways." Her fingers played with the rebel-long strands of hair at the nape of his neck, and she tipped her head to the side. She smiled up at him flirtatiously, that lush mouth of hers displaying a wealth of erotic potential. "What is it going to take to change your mind about posing for my calendar?"

So, they were back to that again. "Absolutely nothing." He released a long exhale just as an idea entered his mind, one that would benefit them both and finally end this agonizing situation for him. "Why don't I just write you a substantial check, donate it to your charity, and we can leave it at that?"

"I don't want your money, Adrian," she said softly, and glided her hands along his shoulders and down to his chest in a too arousing caress. "I want *you.*"

Her words held a dual meaning, one that encompassed her pursuit of him for her calendar and the other holding a more seductive, sexual connotation. He'd like nothing more than to take her up on that second offer, to finally slake the lust that had been riding him hard for the past hour and was increasing with each slow, rhythmic slide of her body along the length of his.

And if he wasn't careful, that lust was going to overrule his common sense. "You'd be better off taking the money, sweetheart, because that's all you're getting from me."

She mulled that over for a moment. "Tell you what, I'll make a deal with you."

He had to admit that he was curious to hear what she had to say, not that he'd agree to any kind of compromise. "What kind of deal?"

Her gaze captured his and searched deep, past those emotional barriers he'd erected and seemingly touching a piece of his soul in the process. "Tell me what you're really hiding from, and maybe I'll back off."

Adrian's lungs squeezed tight, making normal breathing difficult. How the hell she'd managed to hit him where he was most susceptible, he didn't know. And he wasn't about to stick around to find out, either. Needing to get away from Chayse and her too-accurate intuition, he released her abruptly, pulled her arms from around his neck, and headed toward the men's room without looking back.

Once inside and certain he was alone, he slammed his fist against one of the steel doors, which did nothing to dissolve the reckless frustration gripping him—sexual and otherwise. He paced the length of linoleum floor like a caged animal, hating how Chayse so easily threatened his restraint when he was a man who prided himself on control—in his life, with his job and business, and especially with women.

At least until her, he acknowledged and shoved his hands through his thick hair. Now he was constantly grappling for the upper hand between them and battling an upheaval of emotion he had no use for. And the last thing he wanted or needed was the complication of a woman who got to him on such an innate level.

He heard someone enter the restroom and turned around, stunned to find Chayse standing just feet away from him. She locked the main door as if to keep him from bolting again, then leaned against it.

He jammed his hands on his hips and summoned his most intimidating scowl. "Just in case it's escaped your notice, you're in the men's restroom."

She ignored his sarcasm, and that direct, probing look was back in her eyes again. "Mia mentioned that your brothers nicknamed you The Wilde One because you've always taken sports and other adventures to the extreme. Is that true?"

"Yes." Uncertain what she was getting at, he waved an impatient hand between them. "What's your point?"

"How wild and daring are you *really*?"

Furious at her audacity in challenging his manhood, he slowly closed the distance between them until he was looming in front of her. The little spitfire was attempting to pressure him, trying to eventually break him down so he'd give her what she'd been wanting from him for the past four months.

It wasn't going to happen.

He flattened his hands against the door on either side of her shoulders, trapping her against a hard slab of wood and his taut, unyielding body. His mouth twisted with a perverse smile. "Wouldn't you like to know just how daring I am?"

Instead of shrinking back from the bite in his tone, she lifted that stubborn, defiant chin of hers. "Yeah, I would, because it seems to me you're not quite living up to that risk-taking reputation of yours."

Because he wasn't willing to do her calendar. He inhaled a deep breath, his nostrils flaring. God, she was bold and brazen and incredibly brave to provoke him when he was feeling so hot, edgy, and resentful. "Well, let me show you just how wild and extreme I can be."

Before she could so much as utter a comeback or realize his intent, he captured her mouth with his. Her lips parted as she sucked in a quick, startled breath, and he shoved his fingers into her hair and held her head in his hands, rendering her immobile as he delivered a demanding, opened-mouthed, tongue-tangling kiss she couldn't escape.

Knowing how tough and obstinate she was, he wasn't at all gentle with her, determined to instigate a bit of uncertainty in that confidence of hers so she'd back off. He was also hell-bent on making sure she knew what he wanted from her, what he'd greedily take given the opportunity—*her body*. He shifted closer and poured everything into the hot, ruthless kiss—aggression, dominance, and the desperate need to purge her from his mind, his dreams, his entire system.

Fire pooled in his belly and lower, his anger mingling with an undeniable need to possess her in every way imaginable. She didn't resist him as he continued to consume her mouth the same way he wanted to ravish her body, with his lips, teeth, and tongue, and the craving for her grew stronger, a ravenous heat and hunger he was hard-pressed to keep at bay.

His thick erection nudged her mound, and he slid a muscular thigh up between her legs until his knee pressed against her sex, forcing her to ride him. God, he'd never, ever needed a woman as badly as he ached for Chayse. Despite how she aggravated him, he wanted to worship her with his hands, taste her everywhere with his tongue until she begged him to let her come. Then he wanted to fuck her until she screamed with the pleasure of it, and he finally gave himself over to the hot, pulsing release he'd denied himself for too long.

She shuddered and moaned, and it was the pressure of her fingers digging into his arms that snapped him out of his carnal thoughts. He immediately let her go and stepped back so he wasn't crushing her against the door, so that he wasn't wrapped so intimately around her. They stared at one another, both of them breathing hard, panting. Her violet eyes were wide and dilated, her expression stunned and just a tad bit uncertain.

He should have been gratified that he'd finally managed to crack that resolve of hers, but instead, his gut twisted with contrition for his barbaric behavior. He'd never treated a woman so roughly before, not that she'd tried to stop him. No, she'd let him have his way with her, accepting his penchant for being assertive and in control.

While he still had her off-balance, he pressed his advantage. "If you insist on getting those pictures, you're going to have to spend the weekend alone with me at my cabin to get them. And I can just about guarantee that if *you're* enough of a risk taker to join me, we'll finish what we started here tonight. Are you willing to take that chance?"

Still seemingly dazed by all that had transpired, she shook her head and whispered, "No."

He unlocked the door and eased it open for her. "Didn't think so, and trust me, you'll be better off, in every way, finding someone else to pose for your calendar."

For the first time ever, she issued no argument and slipped out of the bathroom and, most likely, out of his life. Just as he wanted.

He ought to be overjoyed at accomplishing his goal. Unfortunately, the victory left a bitter taste in his mouth and generated yet another unwanted emotion … regret for what might have been.

Chapter Two

Adrian wasn't going to be happy to see her, of that Chayse was certain. Lying in the large hammock secured to the thick porch posts of his family's small, cozy cabin while waiting for her outdoor man to arrive, Chayse basked in the warmth of the early-morning sun on her face and bare legs. She was more than prepared to deal with his wrath, more than willing to spend the weekend with Adrian to get the pictures she wanted, and ultimately rise to his dare and show him just how much of a risk taker *she* could be.

Especially after chickening out with him the evening before.

Chayse winced at the recollection of how she'd bolted so cowardly, a moment of weakness she didn't plan to repeat. After spending most of the night berating herself for letting Adrian intimidate her with the hottest, most provocative kiss she'd ever experienced, she'd gotten up early this morning, her resolve rejuvenated and her fortitude stronger than ever. She hadn't gotten through life by shrinking from a confrontation or allowing anyone to coerce her into backing down from something that mattered to her.

She'd learned the valuable lesson of being strong and determined at the age of fourteen, after the death of her ten-year-old brother, Kevin. Her mother's emotional withdrawal had followed, and her parents had ultimately divorced, leaving her floundering for a place to belong. She'd learned to depend on no one but herself and developed the courage to take chances and fight for what she believed in or wanted. And she believed in this calendar project that was a tribute to her brother, and she wanted Adrian's gorgeous face and sexy body to grace not only the cover but the pages within.

She breathed the crisp, cool spring air, knowing she could have found another outdoor man to take Adrian's place. It sure would have been a much easier task than going head-to-head with The Wilde One himself—and she'd almost given up on him for good after he'd rattled her senses with his kiss last night.

There was also her own burning curiosity about Adrian and his true reasons for refusing her request time and again. She knew he was hiding something. She'd always had an eye for that kind of thing, for seeing deeper than the surface. She supposed that uncanny ability came from being a photographer, of being able to really look into a person's eyes or read his or her body language and recognize subtle nuances that nobody else seemed to notice. Adrian was much too defensive about a photo shoot most men would have fun doing in the name of charity, and she was here to discover why. She'd always relished a good challenge, and Adrian was one big, complex puzzle that intrigued her.

She was back in the ring for another round, and this time she was doing so with a clear understanding of the ultimatum he'd given her. That if she made the decision to pursue him for the photos she wanted, not only was she going to have to spend the weekend alone with him, but there would be a heck of a lot more going on between them than picture taking.

A shiver stole through her, puckering her nipples against her ribbed tank top and eliciting a tumble of excitement in the pit of her belly. Oh, yeah, she knew and accepted his terms, and she was perfectly aware that her unexpected presence was the equivalent of handing herself over to him on a silver platter—naked and his for the taking. Willingly so.

She hadn't had sex in a good long time, and if the chemistry that had ignited between them last night was any indication, she was in for one heck of a wild, satisfying weekend. And in the end, they'd both leave this cabin having gotten exactly what they wanted from each other—a win-win situation, in her estimation.

The thought put a smile on her face, and with the

push of her sandaled toe against the porch railing, she set the hammock into a slow, relaxing swing. She sighed and closed her eyes, saturating her senses with the sounds of chirping birds and the rush of water flowing through the creek that ran alongside the cabin. She couldn't help but envy Adrian for having such a peaceful place to escape to, a hideaway retreat tucked away just outside of the Kankakee River State Park and surrounded by trails and trees and craggy rocks. She appreciated Mia giving her the directions she'd needed to get here and surprise Adrian.

The rumbling sound of a vehicle driving up the dirt road leading to the cabin interrupted her peaceful interlude, and she opened her eyes to see Adrian's red jeep appearing around a bend in the road. He came to a long, skidding stop in front of the cabin, creating a billow of dust that settled over her just-washed Honda Accord. With his fingers wrapped tightly around the steering wheel, he remained perfectly still and stared up at her in shock, as if he couldn't quite bring himself to believe she was for real. She grinned and waggled her fingers in greeting, making sure he realized she was no figment of his imagination.

She saw him close his eyes, take a deep breath, then slide from the driver's side of the jeep. He walked to the back of the vehicle and grabbed a duffle bag with one hand and two plastic sacks of groceries with the other. Then he headed toward the cabin.

That he wasn't happy to see her was an understatement. The man was downright furious, and he didn't have to say a word to express his simmering anger. The tense set of his body, his clenched jaw, and his fuming silence said it all.

Despite the sudden rapid beat of her heart, she remained right where she was—on the hammock, waiting to take her cue from him. He climbed the steps, and without so much as looking her way or acknowledging her, he unlocked the door and entered the cabin with the screen door slapping shut behind him like a gunshot. The loud sound made her jump and question the wisdom of infringing upon his male domain.

She immediately pushed that thought out of her head. She would *not* let him intimidate her this time.

A moment later, he came back out, and still ignoring her, he returned to his jeep to retrieve more bags of groceries. Once again, he entered the cabin without so much as eye contact, treating her as if she didn't exist. As if maybe, if he didn't acknowledge her, she'd go away.

Nope, not a chance.

She'd expected him to verbally vent his displeasure, but his silent treatment and his barely restrained temper were almost worse than him just getting pissed at her and letting it out of his system. And sooner or later, she had no doubt his control would snap, and he'd vent all that resentment shimmering off him in waves.

Hearing him moving around inside, making no attempt to deal with the woman waiting for him on the porch, she realized she had two choices—to leave and forget about Adrian or face the gorgeous, moody Adonis inside and let him know she was here to stay. Since going back home wasn't an option, she headed down to her car to retrieve her overnight bag and camera equipment and prepared herself for a confrontation.

It took her two trips to bring everything inside, and she set her belongings in the living room. The cabin was small but well-kept and nicely furnished in oak, beige tones, and hunter-green accents. In a sweeping glance, she was able to see the entire layout of the place. Two doors led to two separate bedrooms, one that looked slightly larger than the other. There was a bathroom and a cozy dining area that adjoined to the kitchen.

Knowing Adrian was putting away his groceries, she headed in that direction. Her sandals clicked on the polished wood floor, announcing her presence, but he didn't turn around and kept stocking the shelves with canned goods.

That was okay by her, for the moment, since his backside was especially fine to look at. Leaning against the doorframe, she eyed him from a professional standpoint, as a subject she'd be photographing. But it didn't take long for feminine instincts to take over, and soon she was studying him as a man in his prime, physically and sexually.

He had an amazing body, athletic and honed to perfection from his business that catered to extreme sports enthusiasts and outdoor adventurists, and his hands-on dedication to rock climbing, rafting, and skiing in the winter was obvious. He was tall, with wide shoulders that tapered to a lean waist. Faded, well-worn jeans hugged his tight ass and strong-looking thighs. There wasn't an ounce of excess fat on his lean, muscled frame, from what she could see.

He wore his pitch-black hair longer than was stylish. The thick, glossy-looking strands were tousled around his head from his drive in his open-air jeep, adding to his bad-boy appeal. The man was outdoor rugged and a little rough around the edges, pure sex and sin in one breath-stealing package. An untamable rebel who tempted her to take a walk on the wild side with him.

If only he'd acknowledge her.

Tired of his silence, she opted to lighten the atmosphere. "The hospitality around here sure is lacking."

"If you want to be waited on, I suggest you go stay at the St. Claire." Finished stashing the perishables in the refrigerator, he twisted the top off a bottle of orange juice and chugged half the contents.

The St. Claire was one of Chicago's finest hotels and far beyond what her budget could afford. "Okay, so there's no bellman to help bring in my bags or room service to make my meals. I can live with that. I swear I'm not high maintenance at all. In fact, I don't need much—"

He spun around so quickly she lost her train of thought and her ability to speak. His intense blue eyes bored into her, searing her with that burning look. "*What* are you doing here?"

She thought that would have been obvious, but it was clear he'd never anticipated that she'd actually take him up on his offer. It was nice to see *him* off-balance for a change. "If I remember correctly, you invited me here."

He set the bottle of orange juice on the counter with a loud *thunk*. "If I remember correctly, you said *no*."

"I changed my mind." She shrugged her shoulders and felt her breasts rise and fall with the movement. "A woman's prerogative and all that."

High color slashed across his cheekbones, and his lips flattened into a grim line. His gaze raked down the length of her body, taking in her tank top and drawstring shorts in that one scathing glance, making her feel as though he'd stripped her naked. His eyes lingered on her chest, and in response, her breasts swelled, and her nipples tightened. She wasn't wearing a bra. She wasn't so huge that she needed one all the time, and since she'd never liked the feeling of being confined, she went without a bra whenever she could get away with it.

She refused to cross her arms over her chest like a timid virgin, and he made no attempt to conceal his hot, hungry gaze, or the impressive erection making itself known behind the fly of his jeans. He'd made it abundantly clear last night that he wanted her body, and obviously a night's sleep hadn't changed his mind.

"How did you find this place?" he demanded gruffly. "For that matter, how did you even know this is where I'd be?"

She figured she owed him that much of an explanation. "I called Mia, and since she didn't know how to get here, she called your brother Steve, and he was nice enough to give her directions, which she passed on to me."

He scrubbed a hand along his taut jaw. "I'm going to kick his ass when I get home," he muttered.

"He was only being helpful."

"He's overstepping boundaries when this is none of his business." He pointed a finger at her, his defenses flaring again. "As for you, you wasted a trip, so you might as well take that sweet little ass of yours back to Chicago before I decide you're fair game."

A tiny thrill shot through her, bolstering not only her desire for this man but her fortitude, as well. She was beginning to understand Adrian well enough to realize he was trying to instill a bit of fear in her with his words, and eventually, his actions. But she was ready to take whatever he dished out and give back as good as he delivered.

"I don't consider my trip here wasted. Not according to the ultimatum you issued me last night." She smiled confidently. "I believe you told me that if I wanted the pictures, I was going to have to spend the weekend alone with you here at your cabin to get them. Well, here I am. I'll honor my end of the bargain if you honor yours."

"God, you are the most thick-headed woman I've ever met!" He slashed a hand between them. "You just don't get it, do you?"

"No, I don't get your resistance at all." And she desperately wanted to understand his reasons.

He stalked toward her, slow and predatory-like, his expression as dark as a summer storm. "You don't want me for your calendar."

She released an exasperated breath. "I wouldn't have come this far if I didn't." She shook her head, and the swish of her hair tickled her neck. "Mia told me you're one of the kindest, most caring and giving guys she knows, and even she can't understand why this is such a problem for you."

He stopped less than a foot away, the heat and male scent of him overwhelming her thoughts, arousing her body, and creating a heavy, tingling sensation between her thighs. The man's ability to turn her on, even during a confrontation, was nothing short of amazing. Then again, Adrian was an amazingly sexy guy who'd been a part of her most erotic fantasies for months now.

He didn't reply, just glared and remained quiet, emanating a sexual kind of tension that seemed to increase with each passing second between them.

"Give me a solid reason why you can't do this calendar project for me," she said, pushing him for an answer even while she resisted the urge to reach out and touch him, to see if she could shatter that control of his. Instead, she provoked him with the only arsenal she had at hand—her words. "Quit skirting whatever it is that has you so bent out of shape, and convince me that I need to find someone else."

"You want a solid reason?" He was literally in her face, his tone low and furious as he yanked the hem of his gray T-shirt from his jeans. "I'll give you *three* reasons why you need to turn tail and get the hell out of here and find yourself another *willing* guy."

In one smooth move, he turned around and ripped his shirt over his head and tossed it onto the counter. For a moment, she was confused, and then she gasped in startled surprise when she noticed that his beautiful back, sculpted from outdoor sports and physical labor, was marred by two long, thick, healed scars that slashed from his left shoulder down to the middle of his back.

"That's two reasons," he bit out and faced her again, his hands quickly unbuckling his belt, unfastening the button to his jeans, and easing down his zipper just low enough for him to tug down the waistband of his pants and briefs to show her yet another imperfection. "And here's your third reason."

She swallowed hard and glanced down, following the black line of hair that bisected his abdomen, swirled around his navel, and arrowed down to his groin. Somehow, despite the raging arousal straining against the confines of his underwear, he managed to remain decent. But at the moment, it wasn't his erection that captured her attention, but instead, her gaze was riveted to yet another line of red, puckered skin that started just above his hipbone, traveled inward, and ended only inches away from the most masculine part of him.

"Satisfied?" he drawled in a mocking tone.

She lifted her gaze back to his face just in time to see a glimpse of guarded emotions before they were chased away with a scowl. There was a story behind those scars, she was sure. One that encompassed a whole lot more than sustaining a physical injury. Those wounds might have healed, but she was betting there were other memories that were still fresh and raw, which was the cause of those barriers he'd erected between them, along with his defiant anger. She ached to know what had happened but knew now wasn't the time to press that particular issue.

"Adrian," she breathed, not sure what to say for pushing him to this extreme but unable to regret finding out the truth. "I'm sorry."

"I don't want your pity or sympathy." He paced away from her, not bothering to zip up his jeans, and those scars on his back shifted and bunched with every move he made. "I just want you to leave me the hell alone."

She just bet he did, but he'd done nothing to convince her to find another guy for her project. She still wanted Adrian and all he represented. Strength, athleticism, along with an untamable wildness that would prompt a whole lot of women to purchase the calendar.

She followed behind him, uncaring that she was crowding his personal space. "I don't pity you. You wanted to shock me, and you did, because that was the last thing I expected. But those scars don't change my mind. In fact, they make you human and give you a sexy edge that makes you all the more appealing."

He turned back around, his expression a mixture of incredulity and anger. Her traitorous gaze was once again drawn to the scar on his hip that now disappeared into the waistband of his briefs. His entire body vibrated with aggression, like a high-voltage wire just waiting to snap.

Slowly, she reached out and glided the pad of her finger along the beginning of the scar. He flinched, and before she could trace the length, he grabbed her wrist and yanked her hand away but didn't let her go.

"*Don't.*" A muscle in his cheek ticked, and he pressed his thumb against the rapid beat of the pulse in her wrist.

She frowned, wondering if the injury still caused

him pain. "Does it still hurt?"

"*You* make me hurt," he said huskily and released her hand. "And if you touch me again, if you stay, then consider yourself touched in return."

The threat was inherently sexual and wholly exciting. This time, Chayse knew exactly what was in store for her and was prepared to accept the consequences of her actions. Holding his gaze, she brazenly stroked her fingers along the scar, blatantly touching him. Daring him. "Then do it, because I'm not leaving until I get what I came here for."

In a lightning-quick move, he lunged at her, buried his fingers in her hair, and pressed her up against the refrigerator with his hard, undeniably aroused body. With a low growl encompassing both frustration and urgent need, he slanted his mouth across hers and sank his tongue deep, kissing her just as recklessly as he had the night before. His mouth promised sin and unrestrained, carnal pleasure, and she matched him stroke for stroke, chasing his tongue with her own, letting him know that she was with him all the way.

The feverish intensity between them was sizzling hot, the strength and immediacy of her arousal making her knees weak. She slid her arms around his waist and skimmed her hands down to cup his buttocks through soft, worn denim. The muscles tightened under her palms, and the long, hard length of him pushed insistently against the crux of her thighs. She felt the bite of his belt buckle against her hip, but she was too swamped with the desire and need coiling tighter and tighter within her to care about the minor discomfort.

With his lips still devouring her mouth with aggressive, utterly devastating kisses, he shoved the hem of her tank top up impatiently, baring her naked breasts to the cool air in the cabin. She shivered and moaned as his big, warm hands closed over her breasts, rubbing and massaging the small mounds of flesh, then rolled her hard, sensitive nipples between his fingers.

He broke their kiss, lowered his head, and closed his mouth over her taut, aching breast. He laved her nipple with his tongue before nipping with his teeth, then sucked her strong and deep, until she felt that same seductive, pulling sensation in the pit of her belly. An electric jolt zapped through her, exploding in heated ripples that thrummed across her nerve endings.

Her skin tingled everywhere, hot and alive with sensation. She twined her fingers in his soft, thick hair, feeling breathless and dizzy and unable to do anything but hold on, let him have his way with her body, and give in to the four months of wild, pent-up passion between them.

He wedged his foot between hers, widening her stance. One hand left her breast and slid down her ribs to her belly. Reaching the waistband of her shorts, he unraveled the tie with a quick yank, loosened the drawstring, and let her shorts drop to the floor.

She sucked in a quick breath, and her heart raced in anticipation as his hand slid between her thighs and his mouth returned to hers, hot and hungry and demanding, allowing her no escape. His fingers skimmed along the leg opening of her panties, and then they were edging under it, delving through damp curls and gliding along the soft, swollen lips of her sex.

A blunt finger slipped easily into her, followed by a second that seemed too much to take all at once. She whimpered into his mouth and stiffened, but then his thumb pressed against her clit, right where she needed his touch the most, both soothing and arousing her at the same time.

As soon as she relaxed, he pushed deeper, filling her, and her inner muscles clamped tightly around his fingers, resisting the invasion. Her head rolled back against the wall, and she panted for air, wondering how she was going to be able to take all of him when the time came.

His big body shuddered, and he buried his face against her neck, his ragged breath hot and damp against her skin. "You are so fucking tight, so hot and wet," he rasped in her ear. "I want inside you."

Wanting that just as much, she gave him her answer. "*Yes.*"

He withdrew his fingers, and she actually mourned the loss, until he slid his hands beneath her bottom and lifted her off her feet. As if they'd done this a dozen times before, she automatically entwined her arms around his neck, locked her ankles at the base of his spine, and held on tightly as he carried her toward the bedroom.

Once inside, he dropped her down on the soft comforter covering the bed, the light in his eyes possessive and bright with lust as he dragged her panties off, nearly ripping them in his haste to get her naked. He left her tank top bunched above her bared breasts, and with quick, urgent movements, he shoved his own briefs and jeans down to his thighs, freeing his full, thick erection. Before she could look her fill, he was pushing her legs wide apart, and his dark head dipped down. The feel of his hot, damp mouth on her inner thigh shocked her, along with the scrape of his teeth and the swirl of his tongue as he burned a sensuous path up to the pulsing, aching core of her.

She moaned as he licked her clit in a hot, searing stroke. Seemingly ruthless in his quest to make her come, he closed his warm, wet mouth over her and plunged his tongue deep. The pleasure was sharp and riveting and stole her breath. A low throbbing began in her belly, then spiraled down to her sex, and she grabbed handfuls of his hair wanting more, needing more…

The sleek, gliding pressure of his thumbs caressing her soft lips and stroking her rhythmically, combined with his wicked tongue working its own seductive magic, was the most erotic sensation she'd ever experienced. Unable to hold back, she let out a cry and arched sinuously against his mouth as she came in a burning wave that shook her entire body.

Without giving her a chance to fully recover from her orgasm, he moved up over her, the slide of his muscled body against hers making her pulse leap higher and faster. She reached down to touch him, and when her fingers fluttered over the broad, velvet head of his shaft, he sucked in a hissing breath. Grasping both of her wrists, he pulled her arms up and pinned them above her head, giving him complete control of the situation.

He settled more fully on top of her, his thighs forcing hers farther apart, and then he was pressing his erection intimately against her, nudging his way in, stretching her, setting her body on fire. She caught a glimpse of his dark, fierce expression before he crushed his mouth to hers and kissed her deeply, passionately. She tasted herself on his lips, on his tongue, just as he buried his shaft to the hilt in her slick heat, possessing her completely.

Their moans mingled, and once he began to move, there was no stopping him, and she instinctively knew there wasn't going to be anything slow or gentle about this first joining. No, judging by the sexual energy and potent heat radiating off him, she prepared herself for a fast, hard, unrestrained ride.

And that's exactly what he gave her. He plunged into her, fast and deep and strong, a rich, seductive rhythm that pulsed as vitally as her heartbeat. His hips ground against hers with each driving, impaling thrust until she felt him go rigid and his lower body arched into her high and hard, pushing her up and over yet another crest. She came again in a blinding climax of intoxicating speed and delirious sensation.

This time, so did he. A low growl erupted from his chest and vibrated against her lips as his body jerked violently against hers, and he finally succumbed to his own blistering orgasm.

More reluctantly than he cared to acknowledge, Adrian withdrew from Chayse's warm, soft body, rolled to his back beside her, and slung his forearm over his eyes, wondering if he'd ever be the same again. His lungs felt tight, his breathing choppy, as though he'd run a marathon. Blood pounded in his temples, and his heart raced a mile a minute. He felt completely drained and totally wasted—four months of frustration and desire and lust finally spent on the one woman he'd craved for just as long.

What the hell had he been thinking to carry her into the bedroom, pin her to the mattress, and take her like some wild man? Problem was, he hadn't been thinking, at least not with the head on his shoulders. No, he'd been so caught up in Chayse, the scent that was uniquely hers, the softness of her skin beneath his hands, the taste of her on his tongue, and the gripping need to drive inside her and make her his. At that moment, nothing else had mattered.

Never had a woman affected him on such a primitive, I-need-to-get-inside-you-now level, but Chayse had that effect on him since day one, and he supposed it was just a matter of the right time and opportunity before they acted on their mutual attraction. Their confrontation in the kitchen had provided such an opportunity, and when she'd made the mistake of challenging him, then boldly caressed the scars he'd bared to make her back off and leave, that's all it had taken for him to unleash the fiery hunger smoldering beneath the surface of his anger.

As the cool air in the cabin rushed over his heated skin and half-naked body, a stunning realization hit him like a sucker punch to the stomach. *Holy shit.* He'd taken Chayse without protection, which said a helluva lot for his state of mind since not wearing a condom during sex was literally sacrilegious for him. There had even been times he'd refused because he hadn't had one on hand.

Not so today. And it was an issue he couldn't ignore, for either of their sakes.

He came up on his side and gazed down at her, still lying where he'd left her minutes before, looking just as wiped out as he'd been. Her eyes were closed, and her hands were still above her head where he'd anchored them, her shirt still bunched high on her chest. Her breasts rose and fell with each deep breath, her nipples tight and just as flushed as the rest of her naked body.

She looked … *beautiful*, and he wanted to touch her again, caress her soft, warm cheek with the back of his knuckles and smooth her disheveled hair away from her face. That bit of tenderness weaving through his system startled him, and he dismissed the thoughts filtering in his mind before he followed through on them.

He wondered if she was sleeping, or if maybe he'd been too rough with her, too demanding, and she was trying to recover. Lord knew he'd taken her with little finesse and a whole lot of sexual aggression, and that knowledge sparked a bit of worry.

"Chayse?" he murmured gently and did what he'd sworn he wouldn't do again—he touched her, trailing his fingers over the slope of her shoulder and down her arm. "You okay?"

She turned her head his way, and her lashes fluttered open. And when a sated, sexy smile curved her lips, it was all he could do not to pull her beneath him again for another round.

"I'm okay," she said huskily and finally pulled her tank top back down over her pert breasts—not out of modesty but, he suspected, because she was chilled without his body heat to warm her.

"Look…" He drew a deep breath before saying, "I didn't use protection."

As if moving in slow motion, she sat up, reached for her panties, and pulled them up her legs and over her bottom. "Don't worry," she reassured him. "I'm on the pill."

He nodded, extremely grateful for small favors. "Oh, good."

She glanced at him and combed her hair away from her face with her fingers. "My doctor put me on it almost a year ago for medical reasons … and you're the first person I've been with since then."

She obviously wanted him to know that she didn't do this kind of thing often, and that notion pleased him more than he wanted to admit. Moving to his side of the bed, he stood up and pulled his briefs and jeans back up, feeling compelled to reassure her, too. "I want you to know I'm clean, so no worries there, either."

"Me, too."

He nodded curtly, suddenly feeling awkward and uncertain with her—another first that confounded him when he was so used to emotionless encounters. And damn if he hadn't felt *something* when he'd been deep inside of her. More than sex and pleasure. She'd not only touched his scars but managed to touch his soul, as well. And it had been a very long time since he'd let any woman that close.

"You can use the bathroom in here," he said, pointing to the adjoining door, desperate to escape to the great outdoors and breathe clear, clean air into his lungs instead of the mingled scents of sex and Chayse. "I'll use the one in the other room."

With that, he left her alone, certain after the way he'd treated her she'd get dressed and hightail it out of there and head back to the city, where she belonged. The thought should have relieved him but instead left him with a hollow feeling in his chest.

Chapter Three

Chayse gave Adrian a half hour on his own before deciding it was time for her to fight for her cause yet again. She refused to let him withdraw from her, and she still wasn't taking no for an answer. Nor would she allow him to berate himself for what had just transpired between them. It had been a long time coming and so worth the wait.

She harbored no regrets, except for the fact that he'd bolted so quickly afterward, leaving her feeling much too alone. And that realization startled her, because she'd been on her own for a long time now and was *used* to being alone.

Having changed into a pair of jeans, a baby-doll T-shirt sans bra, and sneakers, she stuffed her shorts, tank top, and sandals into her duffle, her insides still recovering from their very tempestuous joining. And her outsides, for that matter, as well, she thought with a private smile. Her skin felt hypersensitive, her breasts swollen and tender, and her sex still tingled from two of the most incredible, earth-shattering climaxes she'd ever had the pleasure of enjoying. The man had easily discovered her sweetest spots and had used that intimacy to his advantage, and hers.

Grabbing her camera, she headed outside and followed the steady and loud *thwack, thwack, thwack* sound coming from the side of the cabin. She rounded the corner and stopped in her tracks, momentarily mesmerized at the breathtaking sight that greeted her.

Adrian was chopping wood, his back facing her as he set a thick log on the base of a large tree stump, and with a very accurate, downward swing of his axe, he split the limb in two. He tossed the chunks of wood into a growing pile next to the cabin, then he repeated the process all over again.

He was still shirtless, and the sun glinted off his tanned, muscled shoulders and back and made the fine sheen of perspiration on his upper body shimmer with every move he made. His rakishly long hair was mussed from their earlier romp, and the ends curled damply around the nape of his neck. He was sex and sin personified, the complete embodiment of a gorgeous, earthy male in his element.

She couldn't have set him up with better props if she'd tried, or a more perfect backdrop than the craggy rocks, trees, and trails behind him. Lifting the camera, she began taking pictures. This was the real outdoor man she wanted to capture—no pretenses, no stiff pose or fabricated smile for the camera. Just a man at one with nature, a man who enjoyed the sun and the earth and hard, physical labor.

He didn't acknowledge her, even though she knew he must have heard her behind him, gliding closer and the steady click of her camera. She moved to the side, focusing on a profile shot, which would eliminate the red, puckered scars on his back that he seemed so self-conscious of. Instead, she concentrated on his muscled arms, his defined chest and lean belly, and the way those jeans of his rode low on his hips.

She took in his dark hair that fell over his brow, the chiseled cut of his jaw and beautiful mouth that had given her such incredible pleasure. In time, she hoped those lips would curve into one of his trademark Wilde grins, which she'd been lucky enough to glimpse the first time she'd met him. Before he'd realized she wanted him for her calendar project.

She hadn't seen that sexy smile since.

As she continued taking pictures, she read his body language and those subtle nuances she picked up from behind the camera and knew there wasn't much anger left in him. He was releasing a whole lot of frustrated energy, yes, but there was a resignation about him that bolstered her confidence and gave her hope that she had his cooperation from here on.

He stopped chopping wood and finally glanced her way as she snapped another picture. He said nothing, another good indication that he wasn't going to order her away yet again. Not that she'd go. He watched her, his seductive blue eyes intense and searching, as if he was trying to figure her out, who she was beyond the woman with the camera, what drove her ... *and what was she hiding from?*

In that moment, she felt a sudden shift between them. Her pulse leapt, and she realized she didn't like being on the receiving end of such an analyzing stare. For as much as she liked observing and scrutinizing a person's personality and actions from behind her camera, she'd also used that same camera as a shield to her own emotions and soul-deep pain.

She'd always felt safe behind her lens, always peeking in on other people's lives and feelings but keeping her own hidden away. She'd never felt threatened that someone might realize her ploy, and that Adrian might have that ability made her feel too vulnerable. Because while his scars were on the outside in plain sight, hers were inside, buried deep, and she had no desire to allow anyone close enough to unearth them. As a result, her relationships had always been short-lived, with her ending things before they got too serious. Before she gave her heart and opened herself up to the possible loss and rejection she swore she'd never again subject herself to.

She realized Adrian had that power, and it was a realization that shook her to the very core of her being.

Finally, he spoke, and she was grateful for the reprieve from her unsettling thoughts. "I'm sorry for what happened in there," he said, his tone low and sincere, his gaze still watching her.

"I'm not sorry, so don't go and heap guilt on your conscience for my sake." Not quite ready to lower her camera, she took another picture of him, then another. While she wasn't ready to let him look her in the eyes, she had no problem being honest on this particular issue. "I was a willing participant every step of the way, and that was the best sex I've had in a long time."

"Yeah, me, too." The corner of his mouth quirked, the closest she'd gotten to a smile from him in months, and she caught it before it disappeared again.

He tipped his head, and for as much as he'd previously protested her taking his picture, he didn't object to her enthusiasm now. "Are you still planning on staying the entire weekend?" he asked directly.

He wasn't ordering her to leave, and she took that as a very positive sign. "Yep," she replied with absolute certainty and took an upper body shot of him before finally lowering her camera.

His gaze slowly flickered down the length of her then traversed its way back up to her mouth. "Good, because it's going to take me at least that long to get you out of my system."

Shivers of delight rippled through her at the thought of being Adrian's for the weekend, of letting him have his way with her and being able to fulfill a fantasy or two of her own. "I take it we have ourselves a deal?"

The wicked gleam in his blue eyes spoke volumes. "I believe we do."

She breathed a sigh of relief and felt compelled to let him know she understood his reservations, that she wouldn't exploit him in a way that made him uncomfortable. "Adrian ... while a great body is essential for this calendar to draw buyers, it isn't all just about hard bodies. It's also about a certain smoldering look, which you have, a come-hither glance, a tempting smile. Those are the things that cause a woman's stomach to flutter and make her weak in the knees when she looks at a picture of you." He definitely had that seductive effect on her. "I also want you to know that I respect the way you feel about those scars, and I'll take the pictures in a way that won't blatantly display them. I'll even let you have final approval of what shots go into the calendar."

He nodded, his expression one of gratitude. "Fair enough."

Luckily, he looked good from any angle. She nodded toward the pile of wood and strove to lighten the last bit of tension between them. "So, are you done taking out your frustration on those logs?"

He actually laughed, the sound rich and warm, like a fine cognac. "Yeah, I'm done," he said and buried the blade end of the axe into the tree stump.

Oh, wow, an amused, agreeable Adrian was far more potent than the stubborn man she'd been pursuing for months now. Mia had told her that, under normal circumstances, Adrian was charming, carefree, and flirtatious, and it pleased Chayse to see this side of him. To be the recipient of more than just his scowls and resistance.

"I was hoping we could go hiking through some of these trails and I can take more shots of you outdoors, while the sun is still high in the sky," she said.

Hands propped on his hips, he glanced up at the rugged hills surrounding the cabin, then back to her, a glimmer of doubt in his gaze. "You sure you can handle these mountains?"

It seemed he'd already learned how best to provoke her and that she wasn't one to resist a challenge. "Of course I can handle it!"

"All right," he drawled lazily. "Then let's do it."

Two and a half hours later, they returned from their jaunt through the hills behind the cabin. Adrian was running on pure adrenaline, the kind that rushed through his blood after a good, long, hard work-out. And navigating the uneven terrain and steep slopes that made up the trails he liked to hike definitely qualified as strenuous exercise.

He cast an amused glance at the woman who'd accompanied him on the hike. While she was panting for breath, her skin flushed and glowing with perspiration, he felt invigorated and ready to do it all over again.

"Good Lord," Chayse said as she dragged herself up the front steps of the cabin to the porch. "Why didn't you tell me we'd be climbing Mount Everest?"

He chuckled, glad to see she'd found some humor in the situation when most women would have whined and complained once they'd grown tired. Chayse had been a trooper, sucking it up even when he'd noticed how exhausted she was. And that's when he'd headed back home, knowing she'd had enough.

"That was nothing, sweetheart," he said and jogged effortlessly up the steps behind her. "You ought to join me on a rock-climbing expedition sometime."

"Thanks, but no thanks." She collapsed in the hammock, her body sprawled on the netting and one leg hanging over the side. "God, I'm so out of shape," she muttered in disgust. "My legs and thighs feel like Jell-O."

"But you have to admit you got some great shots out there."

Her lashes drifted shut, and she grunted. "Yeah, when you stopped long enough to let me take a few pictures here and there."

"It was purely an incentive to keep you going and make sure you didn't pass out halfway through the hike," he teased and realized that he was smiling. Again. "It was one thing to carry your backpack of photography paraphernalia for you, but no way was I going to heft you all the way back here as deadweight."

Another grunt, which didn't sound all that complimentary.

His grin slid into a frown as he stared at her lifeless form. He'd meant to give her a workout, yes, but maybe he'd pushed her too hard, and that thought prompted a smidgeon of guilt. "You stay put, and I'll go get you something to drink."

"Trust me, I'm not going anywhere," she murmured.

He went inside and dropped her backpack off in the living room before heading to the kitchen for a bottled water for her and a cold beer for him. By the time he returned to the porch, she'd drifted off to sleep and was snoring softly.

Shaking his head at how quickly she'd dropped off, he perched his backside on the porch railing in front of her, twisted off the cap of his beer, and took a long drink of the malted liquor that quenched his thirst and cooled his body.

Unerringly, his gaze drifted to Chayse, at the softly parted lips he'd kissed earlier and ached to do so again, and the disheveled, chin-length, honey-blonde curls falling haphazardly around her face. His eyes lowered to her chest, taking in her braless breasts beneath her T-shirt and the way the small mounds rose and fell from her even, steady breathing. It was hard not to notice her erect nipples, too, which pressed against the cotton material and made him remember how those crests felt in his mouth, against his tongue.

Ignoring the heat settling in his groin, he took

another swallow of his beer and was forced to admit that he'd actually enjoyed being with Chayse during their hike. He'd teased her, and she'd laughed and even provoked him a time or two, herself. She was definitely a woman who could hold her own with words and comebacks, and he'd had a great time sparring with her. And yes, even flirting with her.

With his anger and grudge toward her dissipated and an amenable compromise agreed upon, he'd allowed a few guarded walls to crumble. A smart move or a stupid one, he wasn't sure which, yet, but he believed Chayse when she said she respected him and his feelings regarding his scars and instinctively knew she wouldn't publish any photos without his permission or approval.

With that understanding between them, he'd decided that he wasn't going to fight whatever was between him and Chayse. His attraction to her was too strong to deprive himself of the pleasure of being with her sexually, and she'd made it perfectly clear she wanted the same thing. And he'd discovered during their hike that he flat out *liked* her. She had a good sense of humor and enough spunk to keep him on his toes. He admired her determination and grit, and she was completely dedicated to the calendar project he was beginning to suspect she was doing for very personal reasons that she'd yet to share with him. Then again, he'd never asked her why this project was so important, and he was suddenly very curious to know the answer.

He polished off his beer and decided to go and take a shower, then start fixing dinner. He was just finishing up the steaks on the small outdoor grill he'd set up when Chayse finally woke up from her nap. She sat up in the hammock, combed her hair away from her face with her fingers, and rubbed at her eyes. She slowly stood and straightened, then grimaced and placed a hand at the small of her back, and he could only assume her muscles had tightened up while she slept.

Transferring the meat to a plate, he turned off the propane tank and climbed the steps up to the porch. "Hey, sleepyhead, you planned that perfectly. The steak and side dishes are done, the table is set, and all you have to do is wash up for dinner."

"Wow, impress me with the service around here, why don't you." A sleepy smile curved the corners of her mouth, and her still-hazy violet eyes met his. "The St. Claire has nothing on you."

He pointed the tongs at her, fighting another smile. "And don't you forget it, sweetheart." He held open the screen door for her, then followed her inside.

She washed her hands at the kitchen sink, then met up with him at the small dining table and sat in the seat next to his, her movements stiff and not at all relaxed. She took in the two rib-eye steaks, the rice pilaf, and bowl of salad, then eyed him with mock suspicion. "You have enough here to feed *two* people.

Are you sure you weren't expecting company?"

"The last thing I was expecting was company of any sort," he drawled wryly and forked a steak onto her plate. "Everyone in my family who uses the cabin tries to keep the place well-stocked. There were extra rib-eyes in the freezer, and I defrosted them in the microwave before throwing them on the grill. The rice was from a box in the cupboard, and I bought enough lettuce and fixings at the grocery store on my way up here to make a salad."

She helped herself to the rice pilaf and slanted him a wide-eyed, hopeful look. "Do I get crème brûlée for dessert?"

"Don't push your luck," he said and passed her the salad. "I bought some chocolate fudge brownie ice cream, and *maybe* I'll share it with you."

"Now there's an incentive to be good." She stretched her arm to set the bowl down on a cleared spot on the table and winced and rubbed at her shoulder. "Wow, I can't believe how much I ache all over. You're a hard man to keep up with out there."

"You did well," he said and meant it.

"Thanks." She poured dressing over her salad and added some croutons. "I wasn't about to admit defeat."

He laughed, not at all surprised to find out that she had a competitive nature to go along with all that determination.

A comfortable silence descended between them as

they started in on their meals, and he was amazed how they'd gone from adversaries to friends in such a short time. Not to mention lovers, too. And there was no denying that he preferred their amicable rapport and the draw of sexual awareness between them to the contention of the past four months.

He cut a piece of steak and chewed on the juicy chunk of meat. "So, what's your vested interest in this calendar project? Other than being the photographer, that is."

She raised a brow, seemingly surprised by his question and, possibly, his insight. She took a long drink of the milk he'd poured for her, then asked right back, "What makes you think I have any ulterior motives other than being the photographer?"

There was enough caution in her expression to confirm his hunch, that there was much more to Chayse Douglas than met the eye. Now that they'd established a truce, he wanted to know what drove this woman, personally and professionally. "Because you're very passionate about the project and how it's being developed. Is it all for the kids at the Children's Hospital, or is there a more personal reason involved?"

"Both," she admitted and pushed her fork through her rice pilaf. After a moment of silence, as if contemplating whether or not to elaborate, she finally continued. "My brother, Kevin, died from a brain tumor when he was ten. I was fourteen at the time, and I spent most of my spare time at the hospital visiting him. I also met a lot of the other kids who were in there for other illnesses, some terminal like Kevin's." Her gaze held a wealth of sadness. "I've been involved in other charity events to raise money for the children's ward, but yes, this calendar project is my personal baby."

He placed his hand over hers on the table and gave it a squeeze. "I'm sorry about your brother." He couldn't imagine losing one of his brothers, or any of his cousins, for that matter. They were a tight-knit group, and something like that would have devastated all of them—just as her brother's death had obviously devastated Chayse.

"He was a great kid. Always happy and optimistic, right up to the very end." She ate another bite of her steak and went on. "But I still miss him and often wonder what my life would be like if he were still around, whether my parents would still be together…"

Her voice trailed off and she grew quiet, as if she'd revealed more than she'd intended. "They divorced?"

She nodded, then hesitated for a moment before trusting him enough to divulge more. "After my brother's death, my mother completely shut down emotionally, and she fell into a deep depression and refused to get treatment. My father couldn't handle the situation, so he filed for divorce, went on his way, and ended up marrying another woman."

The hurt in her voice was nearly tangible, wrapping

around Adrian's chest and squeezing tight. For months now, all he'd known was the stubborn woman with the smart mouth and spitfire attitude, and he found himself poleaxed by the vulnerable, lost little girl she'd been and apparently still was deep inside.

"Where are your parents now?" he asked, curious to know the end to this particular story.

"My mother passed away two years ago, and my father is living in Arizona with his wife and new family." She drained the rest of her milk and tried for a nonchalant shrug. "I don't talk to him much, maybe twice a year."

So, she truly was alone. The thought compounded the ache in his chest and made him want to reach out and pull her into his arms and do his best to chase away those unpleasant memories.

She ducked her head, looking stunned and a little embarrassed that she'd spilled so much—to him, no less. "I've never told anyone all that, except for my best friend, Faith."

He wondered if anyone had ever cared enough to ask, which said too much for his own interest in her life and past. "I promise your secret is safe with me." And what a painful one it was, which made his own private past pale in comparison.

They finished dinner, and when she stood to help clear the table, she winced again as her tendons protested the extraneous movement.

Taking the plate from her, he stacked it on top of

his. "Go and take a long, hot shower to help loosen up those overworked muscles. I'll do the dishes."

"Now there's an offer I'm not about to refuse." A playful smile curved the corners of her mouth. "I *hate* doing dishes."

He chuckled and watched her go, refraining from the urge to join her in the shower and help ease those achy muscles and joints in a more hands-on manner. But after their too-serious discussion, he suspected she needed a bit of time by herself to regroup.

Besides, he had the rest of the night to seduce her.

Chayse stepped out of the shower and grabbed a dry towel, feeling refreshed and somewhat relaxed, if not a little off-balance for how easily she'd opened up to Adrian about her past and family situation. It was true she'd never discussed those details with anyone other than Faith, and while she was shocked that she'd revealed so much to Adrian, she had to admit that his genuine interest and undivided attention had prompted her to share. Undoubtedly, those caring traits of his were dangerous to her heart, and she had to remind herself to keep her emotions out of this weekend's equation. They had a deal, one that encompassed pictures for her calendar and great sex, nothing more, and she'd do well to remember that.

She toweled off her body, ran a brush through her damp hair to let the strands air-dry, and changed into the cotton boxer pajama set she wore at night. She headed out of the bedroom, which adjoined directly to the living room, and came to an abrupt stop when she saw how busy Adrian had been in her absence.

An air mattress had been blown up and was situated in between the couch and love seat and was covered with blankets and pillows. Adrian himself was squatting in front of the brick hearth, tending to the crackling fire on the grate. He was shirtless, the way she liked him best, and had changed into a pair of gray cotton sweat pants. He stabbed at a burning log with a poker, and she watched the play of muscles across his broad back, toned and smooth except for those two long scars she'd yet to ask him about. And he owed her after everything she'd divulged earlier.

"Hey," she said, announcing her presence as she moved deeper into the room, drawn to the man and the warmth from the fireplace. "What's all this?"

He tossed another log on the grate, adjusted the screen in front of the fire to protect them from popping embers, and straightened. He turned to face her, his gaze taking in her nighttime attire in a quick glance before returning to her freshly scrubbed face. "I thought you might like to relax by the fire, and I'll give you a back rub to help soothe your abused body."

Her aching muscles rejoiced at his offer, and the rest of her body was equally thrilled at the thought of having his hands all over her. "That sounds wonderful."

"Consider me your personal masseuse for the evening." A boyish smile eased up the corners of his mouth, and her stomach tumbled and her knees went weak. "It's the least I can do since I'm the one who pushed you out there on the trails today."

"So you were," she murmured, realizing just how dangerous a playful, wholly seductive Adrian could be to more than just her senses. The mattress separated them, and, uncertain what he wanted her to do, she asked, "Where do you want me?"

"Now there's a loaded question." His voice was a sexy, teasing rumble, and he crooked his finger at her in a very tempting way. "Come over here, take off your top, and lie face down on the air mattress."

She came around to where he stood, peeled off her cotton nightshirt in one quick movement, and made herself comfortable in the center of the soft, fire-warmed blankets. Cradling her head in her arms, she waited for the glorious feel of Adrian's strong, capable hands kneading away her physical aches and pains.

The mattress dipped by her side, and he sat astride her thighs from behind. He was still wearing his sweat pants, but the cotton material did nothing to conceal the hard ridge of his erection nestling intimately against her bottom as he leaned forward and splayed his big hand on her narrow back, then kneaded his fingers down the tight muscles bisecting her spine.

She groaned low in her throat, sank into the mattress like a limp doll, and melted beneath his firm, knowing touch. "That … feels … sooo good. By the time you're done with me, I'm gonna be putty in your hands."

"God, I hope so," he said huskily and pressed his thumbs against a tight knot right below her shoulder blade. "So tell me, how did you get into photography?"

She buried her face in her arms, which also helped to hide her smile. "Back to me again, huh?"

"What can I say? You intrigue me."

The feeling on that was mutual, much more than was wise. "You do realize, don't you, that turnabout on all this questioning is fair play?"

"Mmmm," he replied noncommittally as his hands continued to work their magic. "I'll deal with that when the time comes."

She'd just bet he would and wondered if he'd willingly tell her all about those scars of his if she asked or evade the subject for the weekend. She planned to eventually find out.

As for the question he'd just asked her, he'd picked a safe topic, one she was comfortable with and didn't mind discussing. "When I was a junior in high school, I took a photography class. By the end of the first semester, the teacher proclaimed me a natural, took me under her wing, and taught me everything I could ever want to know about photography."

She thought back on that teacher's enthusiasm and encouragement and how it had shaped her future.

"Photography opened a whole new world for me and gave me something to focus on when everything at home was falling apart." Painful memories tried to crowd their way in, and she inhaled a deep breath, refusing to travel down that emotional road again. "After high school, I took some courses at a junior college while waitressing in the evenings. From there, I went to work at a portrait studio, but after a few months, I grew bored doing the same thing day after day."

"You like to be mentally stimulated," he guessed and ran his thumbs up the shallow indentation of her spine, all the way up to the nape of her neck, where he rubbed more taut muscles.

She shivered at the sexual connotation to his words. "That, and I like new challenges. Now I do a lot of freelance work for a couple of advertising firms who commission me for brochures and magazine ads and that kind of thing. It pays the bills and keeps me busy *and* stimulated, but someday I'd love to open up my own photography studio and offer a little bit of everything."

He skimmed his palms down her sides, his fingers brushing the plumped swells of her breasts, causing desire and liquid heat to spiral low. "I have no doubt you'll attain that goal."

Her body turned fluid under his hands, and very aroused. "And why is that?" she asked curiously and stared at the fire burning and crackling in the grate.

"Oh, I don't know," he said in a low, mellow baritone. "It might be that stubborn, determined, persistent streak of yours that makes me believe you'll achieve anything you set your mind to. Like convincing me to do this calendar for you."

He moved off her, but before she could protest the loss, he slipped his fingers beneath the waistband of her pajama bottoms and panties and pulled them down her long legs and off. She came up on her elbows and attempted to turn over, but before she could execute the move, he was back, his thighs straddling hers once again to keep her pinned to the air mattress.

This time, he was completely naked, too, his thick erection nestling in the crease of her buttocks as he covered her from behind and aligned his chest and belly against her backside and pressed her back down onto the mattress. He twined his arms around hers, stretched her hands above her head, and wove their fingers together.

She moaned, and her pulse tripped all over itself, the delicious weight and heat of his body against hers instigating a hungry ache through her veins, as slow and lazy as warmed molasses. The man definitely had a thing for being in control, a dominant male who obviously enjoyed being sexually assertive. Not that she minded, since she knew she'd reap the pleasure of all that confident, exciting masculinity.

"Okay, your turn," he whispered, just as his soft,

warm lips touched down on her shoulder, then moved to the side of her neck, making her shiver as his damp mouth and hot breath rushed over her skin and teased the shell of her ear. "Ask me something, anything at all."

He'd just given her the opportunity to turn the tables on him, to inquire about those scars of his, but how was she supposed to focus on anything remotely serious when all she could think about was having him inside her again?

A smile curved her lips, and she decided to play along with this seductive game of his. "Tell me a fantasy of yours."

"God, where do I start?" he murmured hotly in her ear and arched his hips against her bottom, the heat and pressure of his shaft along her buttocks a maddening, arousing sensation. "You've inspired my most erotic fantasies for months now, and in my dreams, I've taken you a dozen different ways. I've imagined taking you from behind like this, your tight little body clutching mine greedily until you scream from the overwhelming pleasure of me stroking deep inside you."

A shudder rippled through her, drugging her mind, her limbs. She wanted that, too. Her sex felt swollen and achy, and she tried to open her legs for him to slip between, but he kept his knees locked tightly against her thighs. Frustration mingled with her rising excitement. "Adrian, please…"

"Shhh, I'm not done telling you my fantasies." Releasing one of her hands, he pushed her damp hair away from her face. He nibbled her earlobe, then swirled his tongue along her neck while his fingers strummed across the plump outer swell of her breast. "I've imagined you sucking me with that soft, sexy mouth of yours, then climbing on top of me and riding my cock while I watch you caress your breasts and make yourself come. That one's a particular favorite of mine."

He was slowly driving her insane, her body strung tight and throbbing for release. And she'd do anything at all to claim the orgasm tingling just out of her reach, fulfill every erotic fantasy he desired if that's what it took to give her body what it craved. "Then let me do it."

"Mmm, maybe I will … in a minute or two."

Obviously, he wasn't done tormenting her, and since she was pinned beneath him, all she could do was let him have his way with her. His flattened hand slid between the mattress and her belly and moved downward, and she almost wept in relief when his long, warm fingers burrowed between her nether lips.

He stroked her sensuously, expertly. "I love how soft you are right here, so wet and sleek. And now that I know you taste like the sweetest nectar, I just want to lap you up."

She moaned as his tongue dipped into her ear, matching the slow, intimate swirl of his fingers. Her breathing quickened as he continued to share darker, more forbidden fantasies in a low, wicked tone, until her mind and body couldn't take any more stimulation and she came on a long, intense orgasm that ripped a hoarse cry from her chest.

He withdrew his hand and moved off her, and she immediately missed his warmth and weight. She heard him throwing a few more logs in the fireplace, then silence descended, except for the crackle and pop from the wood on the grate. It took her a few moments to recover enough to turn over to see where he'd gone. He wasn't far away, and that was a good thing, because she wasn't done with *him* yet. He sat on the floor with his back against the sofa, his legs drawn up slightly, his own body far from sated.

He gazed at her through hooded blue eyes and crooked a finger at her. "C'mere and ride me, Chayse."

It was an order she wasn't about to refuse. Licking her lips in anticipation, she crawled over to him, but instead of immediately climbing on his lap, she decided to put her mouth to good use and make him suffer a little bit before she put him out of his misery.

Settling between his legs, she leaned forward and captured one of his rigid nipples between her lips. She laved the erect nub of flesh with her tongue, and grazed the tip with the edge of her teeth. A groan rumbled up from his chest as she traversed her way lower, spreading hot, wet kisses on his taut, flat belly. The scar on his hip caught her attention, and she caressed the puckered skin with her tongue and heard him suck in a surprised breath in response to her tender ministration. Finally, she came to his thick, straining erection, and even that part of him was as gorgeous and magnificent as the man himself.

She wrapped her fingers around the hard, velvet-textured length of him and felt him pulse in her tight grip. A drop of pre-come appeared, and she smeared the silky moisture over the big, plum-shaped head of his cock.

She had to taste him.

She took him in her wet mouth, his skin hot and salty against the stroke of her tongue. He shuddered and tangled his hands in her damp hair, and she sucked him, taking him as deep as she could, making the fantasy he'd whispered into her ear a hard-core reality. She pleasured him with her mouth, teased him with her tongue, and aroused him to a fever pitch of need that made his entire body shake with the restraint of trying to hold back.

"Oh, Christ," he breathed and frantically tried to tug her back up. "If you don't stop now, I'm gonna come."

Since she still had more lascivious intent in mind before she let him climax, she heeded his warning. With one last irresistible lick along his shaft, she kissed her way back up his body and crawled onto his lap. She straddled his hips with her knees and directed his shaft upward. She was very wet from all their foreplay, and with deliberate slowness she sank inch by inch on top of him, until he filled her completely and her sex stretched tight around his width.

His nostrils flared, and stark male desire heated his eyes. He clutched her waist with his hands and rocked her tighter against his straining body, setting a rhythm she knew would take him quickly to orgasm.

Feeling naughty, and a bit wicked, she grasped his wrists and pulled his hands away. "If I remember your fantasy correctly, you wanted to watch me come like this."

He groaned like a dying man. "I don't know if I can last that long."

Smiling, she pushed his arms to his sides. "I'll make sure you do."

What he obviously didn't realize was that in this favored position of his, he'd given her complete control of his pleasure, of his release, and she reveled in the feminine power that was hers. With him still buried deep within her body, she cupped her breasts in her hands, fondled the small mounds, and rolled her nipples between her fingers before sliding her flattened palms down her stomach and between her splayed thighs.

She made a soft purring sound of pleasure as her fingers slipped between her soft, lush folds, then strummed across her clit. His chest rose and fell heavily, his expression fierce and hungry as he watched her caress herself and perform an erotic lap dance for his eyes only.

She felt the hot, spiraling sensation of an approaching orgasm, and she rocked into Adrian, just enough to increase the friction inside of her and against her sex. She pressed down on his erection, hard and deep, and came on a soft, shivery moan before collapsing against his chest.

"Nice fantasy," she murmured, a smile on her lips.

He laughed, the sound strained as he trailed his fingertips down her spine. "For you, maybe. I'm still hard as a spike."

"Mmm, so you are." She'd left him that way, deliberately so, and wriggled her bottom against his groin, which prompted a low growl from him.

She lifted her head and stared into his blue eyes, bright with firelight and a burning passion she'd never seen in another man's eyes before. It was passion for her, and the knowledge was like an aphrodisiac to her body and soul.

"In the fantasy you told me, you never said anything about *you* coming," she murmured. "But if you ask real nice, I think I might be able to oblige you."

An amused smile made an appearance as he played the game her way. "Make me come, Chayse," he said and nipped her chin, then her jaw, all the way up to her ear. "I need you *real* bad."

She liked the sound of that. "How do you want it?"

"As wild as you can be," he urged.

More than eager to give this man anything he desired, she wrapped her arms around his neck, locked their bodies so that they were meshed from chest to thighs, and let her inner vixen take over. Lowering her mouth to his, she sucked and nibbled his lower lip, and when he opened for her, she slipped her tongue inside in a smooth stroke that matched the roll and glide of her hips against his.

This time when he gripped her hips, she let him, but he allowed her to set the pace, and she moved on him, enthusiastic and shamelessly uninhibited. She felt his thighs tense beneath hers, felt his stomach muscles ripple, and knew he was nearing the peak of his orgasm.

Twining her fingers in his silky, rebel-long hair, she pulled his head back and dragged her damp, open mouth along his throat, then gently sank her teeth into the taut tendons where neck met shoulder and put her mark on him.

He bucked upward one last time, hard and strong, and his groan of surrender in her ear was the sexiest sound she'd ever heard.

Once his tremors subsided, he tipped her back against the mattress so that he was lying on top of her and stared down at her with a crooked but satisfied grin on his face. "I hereby bequeath my nickname of The Wilde One over to you. You've earned it."

She laughed, happy that she'd pleased him. "I'm so honored," she replied, and ignoring the glimmer of adoration in his eyes along with the emotional tug on her heart that warned her she was falling for this man, she pulled him down for another wanton kiss.

Chapter Four

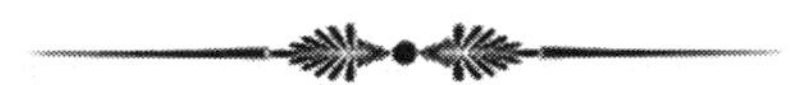

The early-morning sunlight filtering through the living room window didn't provide as adequate lighting as Chayse would have liked, but she wasn't about to pass up the opportunity to photograph Adrian in all his glorious, morning-after sexiness.

She moved silently to the air mattress with her camera in hand and knelt down so she was more on Adrian's level, where he laid sprawled facedown amidst the pillows and rumpled blankets. She probably didn't need to be so quiet, considering the man slept like a rock, and even now, his breathing was deep and measured. No doubt he was exhausted after their night together, and his body was recovering. She, too, had slept soundlessly—once Adrian had allowed her to drift off to sleep, that was. The man had been utterly insatiable, she thought with a reminiscent smile.

Her stomach did a free-fall tumble that had nothing to do with being hungry for breakfast and everything to do with her intense attraction to Adrian. God, the man was so sinfully gorgeous he ought to be deemed illegal. Even asleep and completely mussed, he managed to exude an earthy, sexual magnetism, one she was finding dangerous on so many levels—physically, emotionally, and mentally. The fact that this man had the ability to affect her so completely was a scary prospect she wasn't prepared to face or deal with.

She adjusted the settings on her camera to compensate for the lack of lighting, then glanced back at her subject, taking in his natural pose and the naked slope of his beautifully muscled back, all the way down to where the blanket was wrapped low around his hips. She'd also discovered that Adrian was extremely hot-blooded and didn't require much to keep him warm, whereas she liked to burrow beneath a mound of covers.

Yet their different levels of sleeping comfort hadn't stopped him from reaching for her during the night and tucking her tight against his body. And she'd gone to him willingly, letting his presence fill that vast loneliness that had been such a part of her life for so long. She'd allow herself that luxury, if only for a night or two, before the real world intruded on their weekend affair. And before they parted ways, she wanted to remember him just like this, and these photos would be her private souvenir of their time together.

Lifting the camera and bringing Adrian into crisp, clear focus, she began taking her pictures. Surprisingly, it didn't take long for the clicking sound to rouse him from slumber. Through her lens, she watched him stir and caught his gradual awakening on film. One eye slowly opened, then the other. A dark brow lifted lazily, as did one corner of his sensual mouth.

"Smile, you're on Candid Camera," she greeted softly.

He chuckled, a low, rumbling sound that tickled the pit of her belly. Then he rolled over to his back and stretched the kinks from his long, lean body, and she took advantage of all that naked flesh and those rippling muscles. His glossy hair was tousled in a messy disarray around his head, and dark stubble lined his jaw, making his eyes stand out like twin sapphires. Even the hair in his armpit was silky and sexy-looking.

As he flexed his legs, the blanket around his hips slipped lower on his abdomen, revealing not only his scar but the fascinating trail of hair that led to more delightful treasures. "You better put the camera down before you get some indecent shots," he warned, his tone low and wicked.

"Don't worry, you can get as indecent as you want. These pictures are for *me*." It was then that she noticed the impressive tent his erection had made beneath the covers, and she glanced at him from above her camera in mock reproach. "Why, Adrian, is this photo session turning you on?"

He gazed at her through lashes that had fallen half-mast. "No, *you* turn me on. I can see your nipples through that T-shirt you're wearing, and I vividly remember what those panties are covering."

She shivered, but not from the cool morning air in the cabin. The man had a way with words that made her melt, along with a natural ability to seduce the camera, and her. "Ever thought of posing for *Playgirl*?"

"Not on your life." He looked completely stricken by the very idea. "This beefcake calendar is as far as I go."

She laughed, feeling carefree and flirtatious and enjoying the private, intimate moment between them. One that would always be theirs alone. "You'd make a lot of women really happy."

"I'm not interested in making anyone happy but you."

Her heart stuttered, then resumed at a frantic pace. She told herself she was reading too much into his words, that she'd most definitely misinterpreted the deeper meaning she'd seen in his eyes. "Then you'll be satisfied to know that you made me deliriously happy last night."

"And I can do so again this morning," he drawled, all arrogant, presumptuous male.

And because Chayse had firsthand knowledge that he was a man who more than lived up to his provocative claim, she couldn't find fault with his very confident assumption.

An irresistible smile tipped up the corners of his mouth. "Put down the camera, come here, and let me show you how happy I can make you."

Unable to refuse him anything, or herself, for that matter, she set her camera safely aside and crawled across the mattress to him. "Think you can top delirious, do you?" she taunted playfully.

"Sweetheart, I *know* I can."

He tumbled her onto her back, and before her peal of laughter could subside, he had her shirt skimmed over her head and tossed to the floor and her panties a distant memory, as well.

He pushed her legs apart, moved in between, and slowly stroked his warm, callused palms up her thighs, until his thumbs caressed her intimately. "I think the real question here is, can you survive just how happy I'm going to make you?"

Already, she was trembling in anticipation, and the rogue knew it, too. "There's only one way to find out, now, isn't there?"

"Oh, yeah," he agreed huskily, and she caught a quick glimpse of his I'm-gonna-lap-you-up-until-you-scream grin as he settled himself more comfortably between her legs. He nuzzled her thigh and applied a wet suction to a patch of flesh that made her gasp and would no doubt leave a hickey behind.

"Forget delirious," he rasped once he was done branding her, his tongue now swirling a path to where she ached for his attention the most. "We're going for blissful, ecstatic, and rapturous."

The man was as good as his promise and delivered on all three.

Adrian took Chayse on another long hike, though this one not as strenuous as yesterday's trek. They followed a trail alongside the creek by the cabin that led upstream, which provided plenty of clearings and backdrops for her photos. Today he'd worn a white T-shirt, jean shorts, and hiking boots, and while she'd gotten a couple of shots with his shirt on, it didn't take her long to ask him to strip it off for another round of photographs.

Once she was done with their two-hour session and declared herself starved for the lunch he'd packed, he didn't bother putting his shirt back on. The day was cool, but the sun on his skin felt warm, soothing even. And he was beginning to learn how impetuous Chayse could be when it came to taking pictures, and he figured he might as well be ready for her spontaneous snapshots.

She helped him spread a blanket in a clearing in the sun, and sure enough, she insisted on getting a few pictures of him stretched out on the blanket, arms behind his head, and chewing on a long piece of grass. All he had to do was think about this morning's tryst with Chayse, the hickey he'd put on her thigh, and how many times he'd made her come before he'd taken his own pleasure, and the sexy smile she asked for appeared on his lips.

She took shots from a dozen different angles, and he watched her while she worked, his eyes following the camera as she directed. The woman had so much passion and enthusiasm and applied it to everything she did—from standing up to him and following him to the cabin to get what she wanted, to taking her pictures and even making love. It amazed him that no other man had appreciated all her qualities and snatched her up for his own.

Then again, he guessed that, just like himself, she'd kept the opposite sex at arm's length to protect her emotions, and he understood that safety net she was clinging to because he'd been using one himself for the past four years. Everyone saw him as a carefree, footloose bachelor who loved adventure and thrills. But few knew the man beneath, the one who'd grown cautious and guarded after being burned by another woman.

And now, he was prepared to share that private side with Chayse, because he wanted whatever was between them to last a helluva lot longer than just the weekend. Not just the hot chemistry and great sex, but also the friendship and emotional connection he felt with her that he'd never, ever experienced with another woman. She was his match in so many ways, and after months of denying his feelings for her, he wasn't about to let her go without giving them a chance. And that meant opening up and trusting her with his past.

"Oh, damn, my SD card is filled."

She sounded so disappointed, but a part of him was relieved. Between yesterday and today, she must have taken a gazillion shots, and while he was cooperating in the name of charity, he so wasn't cut out to be a model. "Good, now we can eat." He reached out to where she stood less than two feet away and cupped his hand over her smooth calf, then moved closer and nibbled on her leg with a low, rumbling growl. "I'm so hungry I'm about ready to take a big ol' bite out of you."

She laughed, sidestepping him before he could sink his teeth into that tempting bit of flesh, and sent him a chastising look. "You know, so much sugar really isn't good for your system."

Sugar and spice and everything nice. Oh, yes, she was especially sweet, in every way. "Okay. Lunch first, then dessert." He waggled his brows at her, making sure she knew he considered *her* his dessert.

While she put away her camera, he sat up and reached for the extra backpack with the lunch he'd made for the two of them. He pulled out three ham-and-cheese sandwiches—one for her and two for him—a bag of chips, and two cans of soda. She settled in beside him, and he was done with his first sandwich before Chayse finally broke the compatible silence between them.

"Okay, Mr. Wilde," she said, slanting him a speculative glance. "You owe me."

He raised a teasing brow. "What, *another* orgasm?"

She actually ducked her head and blushed, and he found the gesture very endearing, showing him a softer side to the woman who touched him in long-forgotten places. She'd stood toe-to-toe with him during numerous heated arguments since they'd met, had let go of every inhibition with him sexually, and now she'd been struck by a moment of modesty. This sexy yet vulnerable woman never ceased to intrigue him.

"You've more than made up for that, especially this morning." She took a long drink of her soda, then reached for a potato chip. "Remember turnabout being fair play and all that? It's time for you to pay the piper and answer a few of *my* questions."

He took a big bite of his second sandwich and glanced out at the blue, cloudless sky. He'd known this interrogation was coming, knew in his gut what she was going to ask, and had no intentions of skirting the issue as he had for the past four months with her. It was time to get everything out in the open, to let go of the bad memories and start out fresh and new.

"I'm an open book, sweetheart," he said with an engaging smile. Done with his sandwich, he shoved his empty baggie and napkin back into the backpack. "What would you like to know?"

Her gaze flickered from the puckered skin on his

bare abdomen to his face. "Those scars—how did it happen?"

It wasn't often he thought back to the skiing accident that had nearly killed him and made him realize that not many women were equipped to understand and accept his need for thrills and extreme adventures. "It happened four years ago. Me, a few friends, and our girlfriends took off for a winter vacation in Jackson Hole, and while the women were out shopping for the day, the four of us guys decided to do go heli-skiing."

He saw her confused expression and explained, "That's where a helicopter takes you to the top of a mountain peak in a remote area with virgin snow and untouched terrain. They let you out with a guide, and off you go, down five thousand vertical feet of pure adrenaline rush."

Her eyes widened in shock. "That's absolutely *insane*."

"That's the whole point of extreme sports," he agreed with a laugh. He'd always loved the challenge and risks involved, which made each adventure all the more exciting. "I'd been heli-skiing before, and there's nothing like all that fresh powder, steep slopes, and speed to get your heart pumping and your blood flowing in your veins. Of course, navigating all those jagged peaks, glaciers, and Alpine bowls can be very dangerous if you're not a skilled skier."

Unfortunately, not even his experience, expertise,

and normally quick reflexes had been enough to save his sorry ass that fateful day. "Everything was going great until I skirted too close to the edge of a rocky peak. I dislodged a boulder, and I went down with it. I plunged over the edge of the cliff, right into a ravine, and tumbled a good five hundred feet while being ripped apart and impaled by razor-sharp rocks."

She sucked in a breath and pressed her hand to her heart. "Ohmigod, Adrian…"

He knew the horrifying images his words must have put into her mind, but there was no way around the truth of the matter, so he met her concerned gaze and finished his tale. "Unfortunately, there aren't any safety brakes on this kind of thrill ride," he said wryly. "You just have to hang on and ride it out until the very end. By the time the rough terrain spit me out at the bottom of the mountain, I'd sustained a concussion, four broken ribs, and three deep gouges from the jagged rocks that had ripped through my jacket and clothes, which accounts for the scars on my back and lower stomach."

She shook her head in wonder, and her silky hair grazed her chin with the swift movement. "You're lucky to be alive."

"Wearing a helmet saved my life, I'm sure. Without it, I would have ended up with more than just a concussion." He didn't go into the unpleasant details of that particular scenario, but it was obvious by her grimace that she'd come to her own gory conclusion.

"It also helped that the helicopter was right there to airlift me off the mountain and take me to the nearest hospital. My girlfriend at the time, Felice, was the first person I saw once I woke up."

A long breath unraveled out of Chayse. "She must have been frantic with worry."

"Yes, she was." He drew up his knees, crossed his ankles, and wrapped his arms loosely around his legs. "The accident gave everyone a good scare, myself included, but I wasn't expecting to deal with an ultimatum the moment I opened my eyes. I remember trying to smile at Felice, which hurt like hell, and the first words out of her mouth were a demand for me to choose either her or extreme sports and my business because she wasn't going to stick around if I continued to put my life at risk. Needless to say, she flew back home alone before I was even discharged from the hospital."

"That would be like someone forcing me to give up photography. I could never, ever do that." Her tone was just as vehement as the violet fire flashing in her eyes—all on his behalf. "You made the right choice."

He should have known that Chayse would understand, and he experienced a huge amount of relief that she'd jumped to his defense. "Without a doubt." At the time, it had been difficult to watch Felice walk out of his life, especially when he'd needed her the most. But in the end, she'd done him a huge favor by ending their relationship before he'd grown to resent her constant demands to give up something that was such a huge part of his life.

Chayse reached out and trailed the tips of her cool fingers along the two long slashes on his back, her gentle, intimate touch a balm to his soul. "These scars … they give you character, Adrian. They're a part of who you are and what you do, and always will be."

She understood so much about him, and her acceptance mattered more than he'd realized.

Since his accident, he'd never allowed himself to care what another woman thought of his scars or the extreme adventure business he ran for a living, and it was a huge, shocking revelation to realize that Chayse's opinion mattered the most. With sudden clarity, he knew that was part of the reason he'd avoided her for four long months, because his subconscious had obviously known what his emotions hadn't been ready to face or accept—that this woman who challenged him at every turn, who pursued him despite every attempt he'd made to reject her, and who gave of herself so openly and generously when they made love, could very well be the one for him.

He felt lighter and freer than he had in years, and Chayse was the reason. He glanced at her, met her soft violet gaze, and wanted to tell her everything he'd just discovered himself and how much he wanted her to be a part of his life, but he was fairly certain she wasn't ready to hear something so life-changing. If he'd learned anything about Chayse this weekend, it was that she had her own personal issues to work through and her own past to come to terms with. That despite her outward show of determination and impetuousness, inside she was a woman who was as vulnerable and fragile as fine crystal. And he had to treat those emotions accordingly.

When she leaned toward him and her lips drifted over his shoulder and along those scars of his, arousing and distracting him, he figured he had the rest of tonight and tomorrow to help her work through those issues and state his intentions.

"You know, I'm suddenly ravenous for dessert, and I want to eat it right out here in the great outdoors," he announced, and burying his fingers in her hair, he brought her mouth to his and kissed her, long and slow and deep.

Between wet, leisurely, tongue-tangling kisses, they undressed one another, until they were both naked and the sun dappled their skin with warmth. He pressed her down on the soft blanket, proceeded to feast on every sweet inch of her, and took his time doing so. He lapped in her honeyed essence and touched and stroked her in all the places he knew she liked to be caressed the most, until she was breathless and trembling and begging him to end the sensual torment.

Only then did he drive into her soft, welcoming body, and she automatically arched to take all of him. In this, she held nothing back, and it gave him hope that he'd be able to breach other barriers with her, as well. He reveled in her uninhibited response to him and the way she wrapped her legs around his waist and urged him to a stronger, harder rhythm that sent her soaring.

She came with a soft moan, and only then did Adrian allow himself to let go of his own orgasm and lose himself in everything that was Chayse Douglas.

Chayse curled her feet beneath her on the couch and watched as Adrian tossed a few more logs on the grate and stoked the fire to life. A smile touched her lips as she enjoyed the play of his muscles across his bare back and the way his sweat pants rode low on his lean hips. Her fingers itched to grab her camera to add this sexy pose to her personal collection of candid shots of Adrian, but she managed, just barely, to restrain the urge.

She stifled a sleepy yawn, and even though it was nearing midnight, she wasn't ready to call it an evening just yet. Nor did she want this fun, relaxing weekend with Adrian to end, but she knew that was as inevitable as the sun rising in the morning.

This afternoon and their conversation about his scars had triggered feelings she hadn't expected. She'd meant it when she'd told him she understood his love for his job, for taking risks with extreme sports, but her emotional reaction to his story underscored her fears of getting too close to Adrian and caring whether or not he left her like everyone else she opened her heart up to. And that knowledge scared her enough to cement her decision to make a clean break tomorrow.

As for today, the afternoon had passed much too quickly for her liking, but the memories dancing in her head were ones she'd cherish for a long time to come. They'd returned from their photo session after making love outdoors not once but twice and shared a nice, long hot shower. Then, with a blanket tucked around the two of them, she'd snuggled up to his side, and they'd taken a nap in the hammock. He'd made spaghetti and garlic bread for dinner, then afterward he fed her his chocolate fudge brownie ice cream. They played a few games of cards, drank hot cocoa with marshmallows, and discussed recent movies, books, and other personal favorites.

And then he'd regaled her with amusing tales of his brothers and cousins and his big, large, happy family that made her laugh but also made her all too aware of the fact that she had no lighthearted stories of her own to share in return.

No, her childhood had been emotionally painful and unstable, and there weren't a whole lot of cheerful moments to recall. From the loss of her brother to her mother's withdrawal and depression, to the father who hadn't been there for her when she'd needed him the most. She'd been forced to grow up much faster than any teenager should have to and had learned to guard herself from any more pain and loss by keeping people, and men, at a distance. And so far, those barriers had served her well and had kept her heart protected.

She envied Adrian his close-knit family, the stability and unconditional love and support he'd grown up with. It was something she'd always dreamed of, wished for, but her past was unchangeable, and she accepted that. She'd made the best of the hand she'd been dealt, and she was proud of her accomplishments. She had a thriving photography business, her best friend, Faith, and all the kids who became a part of her life during their stays at the Children's Hospital.

And now there was Adrian, a man who had an effortless way of filling the vast emptiness inside her with laughter and fun and incredible, vibrant feeling.

"Hey, you ready to call it a night?"

Startled from her thoughts, she met Adrian's caring gaze and knew how easy it would be to drown herself and her painful past in those velvet blue depths. But not yet, she told herself. This man had let her into his life in so many ways and had shared his family with her in those humorous, uplifting stories that had given her such a deeper insight to him as a man, a brother, and a son. And while she might not have fun, amusing childhood tales to entertain him with, there was a private part of her life she wanted to share with Adrian in return. A piece of herself she'd never allowed another man close enough to see or be a part of.

"I want to show you something," she said, and before she lost the nerve, she moved off the couch and retrieved a pocket folder from her backpack. Then she joined Adrian on the mattress, crossed her legs, and opened the portfolio.

She spread out a few dozen different snapshots that encompassed people of all ages, genders, and ethnicities, most of which had been taken candidly or with a telephoto lens so as to keep her hobby discreet and avoid rudely intruding on a stranger's life. There were photographs of people at Lincoln Park, others at Navy Pier, and many she'd taken while strolling through the city on a Saturday afternoon. She rarely left home without her camera, and she'd learned that anything could become a photo opportunity at any given moment.

"Did you take these pictures for clients?" he asked curiously.

"No, I took these photographs for my personal collection." He appeared confused as to why she'd take pictures of virtual strangers, and she explained. "When I first started taking photography classes in high school, I'd spend my afternoon and weekends practicing by taking pictures of everything, but I was mostly fascinated by people, because their pictures always seemed to show so much emotion. Taking candid shots turned into a hobby for me, a way to escape the world in which I lived and wonder about the other person's life."

Adrian picked up a photograph she'd taken at a little league game she'd happened by one morning. "How about this little guy? Is he someone you know?"

"Nope. Another casualty of my trigger finger, I'm afraid," she said jokingly. "I was out one Saturday morning and came across this ball game in progress, so I stopped to watch the kids play. This young boy was up at bat, bottom of the ninth with the bases loaded. He was so disheartened after two consecutive strikes, and you could tell he didn't want to disappoint his teammates by striking out and losing the game. No matter the outcome, I knew this was a picture I wanted for my collection."

She smiled, remembering how the boy's expression and attitude had changed to determination and what she'd ultimately captured on film. "On the next pitch, he smacked the ball over the fence, and here he was, still standing at home plate, the bat in his hand, his eyes wide with awe and disbelief as he watched the ball soar through the air. The crowd behind him was standing and cheering, and in a split second, he became the hero who saved the game." She cast Adrian a sidelong glance to gauge his response. "It's one of the neatest photographs I've ever taken."

"It's pretty amazing, actually." He met her gaze, the bright firelight causing his irises to glimmer with blue heat. "I can actually *feel* that kid's excitement."

"Exactly." Elated that his emotions had been

touched by a snapshot *she'd* taken, she sought out another picture to show him. "I was at the mall one day, strolling along the upper level, and I happened to glance down and saw this mother and daughter standing outside an accessory store. As you can see, the girl is showing her mother her new belly button piercing and trying to convince her that it's the in thing, but mom's not going for it."

Adrian chuckled in amusement. "Oh, boy, her mother has that wait-until-your-father-finds-out-about-this look on her face."

Chayse lifted a brow. "And how would you know that look?"

"Because it's a universal look among mothers, my own included," he said with a shrug that made the firelight play along the muscles in his back and arms. "Anytime my mother shot any of us boys *that look*, we knew we were in *big* trouble when Dad got home."

She sorted through more photographs, wishing her mother had cared enough to snap out of her depression long enough to take an interest in whatever her daughter was doing—good, bad, or otherwise. Luckily, Chayse's photography hobby had kept her from turning into an outright rebel with a cause. And Lord knew she'd had *plenty* of cause.

As the fire crackled warmly in the hearth, and with Adrian enjoying her pictures, Chayse continued to entertain him with the stories she saw within the photographs. On some of the snapshots, he even offered his own observations, most of which echoed hers. When she came across a picture she'd taken of a homeless man, her chest tightened with emotion as she remembered that day.

"This is Frank," she said and showed Adrian the five-by-seven shot of a man sitting on a park bench, his clothes old and tattered. His hands were gnarled and dirty, his face unshaven, and he was holding a crude cardboard sign that said *will work for food*. "I took one look into his sad eyes and knew he'd lived a long, hard life. I bought him a hotdog and soda from a vendor in the park, and I sat down to talk to him. Despite how gruff and scruffy he looked, he was a sweet man, and when I asked if he had any family, he told me he'd lost his wife and two kids twenty-three ago in a car accident and that he'd been the sole survivor of the accident. It didn't take much to figure out that the loss had devastated him, to the point that he stopped caring about anything, including his own life."

She brushed her thumb along the edge of the photograph, feeling the man's pain and heartache deep in her chest. "I asked him if I could take his picture, and he gave me permission to do so. He even smiled for me," she said, pointing to the man's gap-toothed grin.

Adrian glanced from the photo to her. "I'd bet you were the bright spot of that man's day."

"I'd like to think that I was. Before I left, I gave him twenty dollars to make sure he had a few more good meals, but he gave me so much more in return." A lump rose in her throat when she thought about her memorable encounter with Frank. "This photo tells a hundred stories, and every time I look at it, I hear a different tale. Crazy, huh?"

Adrian gently tucked wayward curls behind her ear, his expression full of tenderness and understanding, as if he had a direct link to the lonely, vulnerable little girl inside the woman who sought comfort in her pictures of other people. "No, it makes perfect sense to me."

Her breath caught and held, much like her stuttering pulse and the squeeze of her heart that yearned for all the things she'd grown up without. All the things she swore she didn't need in her life but Adrian made her believe were possible.

Fears and insecurities reared their ugly head, and she looked away and began picking up the pictures to put back in the portfolio folder. "Most people read books. I read pictures," she went on in a rush. "And the photos I take outside of the studio are my personal storybook."

"I like that," he murmured, more calmly than she felt.

She knew she was babbling, anything to keep the conversation going. "Sometimes I take certain shots of people, and it's like I have a window straight into their souls." Finished putting away the snapshots, she set the folder up on the couch but couldn't bring herself to look at Adrian again.

But she should have known that he wouldn't let her escape him so easily. His fingers curled around her arm, and he gently tugged her down onto the air mattress, then stretched out beside her, with half his body pressing against hers and a thigh resting heavily between her legs.

He stared deeply into her eyes, so intuitive and determined. "Sometimes people don't need a camera to see into another person's soul," he said and cradled her cheek in his big, warm palm, forcing her to confront the emotional connection between them that scared the living daylights out of her. "I look into your eyes, and I see a little girl who's carried a wealth of emotional burdens for too many years now and a woman who is afraid to take chances on what most likely is a sure thing. I see a woman who hides behind her camera, even while she tries to uncover everyone else's deepest secrets."

She shook her head frantically, trying to deny the painful truth he'd so easily unearthed about her. She'd let him too close, shared things with him she should have kept to herself. "Adrian—"

He pressed his fingers against her lips, quieting her. "You don't need to hide anything from me, Chayse. Ever. I'll always be here for you."

It was those words that she found the hardest to trust in, even though her heart wanted so badly to believe in Adrian—the honorable man he was and the promises he made. Tears gathered in her throat and stung the backs of her eyes. Not wanting him to witness her weakness, her greatest fears, she plowed her fingers through his hair and brought his mouth down to hers.

She kissed him deeply, hungrily, *desperately*, striving for mindless pleasure to chase away her doubts and uncertainties. Sliding her hand down his belly, she cupped his erection in her palm and stroked him through the soft cotton of his sweatpants. She felt him grow and harden from her touch and started to move over him to straddle his waist, needing him in ways she couldn't define. Physical need was a given, but it was all the other emotional chaos swirling within her that made her feel as though her carefully guarded life was spinning out of her control.

He caught her around the waist before she could crawl on top of him and eased her back to his side. She made a small sound of frustration, and he deliberately slowed their kiss, soothing rather than arousing her with the slide of his lips against her soft, yielding mouth. Then he grasped her wrist and rested her palm right over his rapidly beating heart and held it there.

He ended the kiss and nuzzled her cheek, her hair. His shaft pressed against her hip, but it was obvious to her that he didn't intend to do anything about that particular discomfort. "Just let me hold you, Chayse," he whispered in her ear.

She nearly broke down right there, but after years

of being strong and holding herself together, she was conditioned to keeping her emotions locked away tightly. And those honed instincts kicked in now, enabling her to keep her tears at bay.

Still, she couldn't ignore his tender offering. He wanted to hold her. When had anyone ever just held her, without the pretense of anything more? And how did this incredible man know exactly what she ached for, right when she needed it the most?

Tired of pretending that she could face the world alone, she sank against Adrian's side, rested her cheek on his chest, and absorbed the comfort and affection he so selflessly offered her.

She closed her eyes, and as he held her in his embrace and she let his strength take over, she knew this weekend together wasn't about sex anymore. Not for either of them.

Chapter Five

Chayse slept better than she could ever remember and woke the following morning to the familiar sound of a camera clicking. Knowing for certain she wasn't dreaming, she opened her eyes and found Adrian standing at the edge of the mattress, her camera in hand, focusing on her.

Click, click, click.

She frowned, unable to believe that Adrian had been bold enough to turn the camera on her when no one ever had before. And especially after their conversation last night. "What are you doing?" she asked warily.

He flashed her a killer grin that looked positively devious combined with the dark stubble on his jaw. "Getting even."

"Oh, ugh!" She put a hand up to ward him off, but he was a man on a mission and kept taking her picture anyway. "Adrian, I look like a wreck!" And no way did she want to be a part of her private collection.

His dark blue eyes peeked up at her from above the camera, and he waggled his brows. "A beautiful, gorgeous, sexy wreck."

She rolled her eyes at his misplaced flattery. "You can't be serious. I've got a major case of bedhead," she complained, knowing her hair was tweaked every which way.

Undeterred, he refocused on her and snapped another shot. "The politically correct term for bedhead is tousled," he informed her, a teasing note infusing his deep morning voice. "And tousled is *very* sexy."

She laughed at his attempt at humor and forced herself to relax. To not feel so threatened by her own camera. "I'm grumpy in the morning, especially when I wake up to find someone taking my picture." She stuck her tongue out at him to prove her point.

He captured her petulant attitude and pout with a click of his finger. "I can handle grumpy," he assured her and knelt on the mattress to get a close-up of her. "In fact, I know a very good cure for the morning grumpies."

Her body warmed at the provocative, tempting insinuation in his tone. There had been no making love last night, just cuddling, and she suddenly craved him one last time before she left to return to the city. Before she left Adrian behind, which was the right thing to do, because he certainly didn't need an emotionally screwed-up woman like her in his life.

She smiled to cover up the heartache making itself

known and stretched, causing her T-shirt to ride up on her belly and tighten across her breasts. "Tell me more about this cure of yours, Mr. Wilde One."

He paused for a moment to stare at her hard nipples before lifting his heated gaze to hers. "I promise to share my therapeutic remedy, just as soon as you cooperate a little for me. Seduce the camera, and have a little fun with this."

How many times had she told Adrian the very same thing? "I never thought those words could come back to haunt me." Even though the camera unnerved her because she knew what depths a photograph could reveal, she resigned herself to this playful, intimate moment between them.

She made it a game of seduction in her mind, her ultimate goal to make Adrian lose control and forget about taking her picture. First, keeping herself covered with the thin thermal blanket, she peeled off her T-shirt and tossed it aside. Then she wriggled out of her boxer shorts, then her panties, which she tossed at Adrian and managed to land them on his shoulder. He picked up the scrap of fabric, and grinning like the bad boy he was, he brought the silky material to his nose and inhaled deeply.

"God, you smell good," he groaned and breathed in her scent again before dropping her panties to the floor and returning his attention to the camera, and her. "Flash me some skin, sweetheart."

She lowered the covers to the upper swells of her

breasts and slipped one leg out so she was bared to the curve of her hip. Lowering her lashes, she smiled provocatively and gave him a sultry, Marilyn Monroe-like pose that made her feel sexy, despite her bedhead. Before long, she was lost in Adrian's husky praise and coaxing as he continued to capture her seduction on camera, and enjoyed herself and the fact that she was turning him on, too.

Deciding to turn up the temptation a few notches, she rolled to her stomach and let the blanket slide down her back to the base of her spine, so that her bottom was still covered, just barely. Angling her knee so that her thighs were spread beneath the blanket and using one arm to keep her upper body braced, she slid her flattened hand along her belly. She looked over her shoulder at Adrian, her disheveled hair in her face, and slowly glided her splayed palm downward, until her fingers encountered the creamy, wet warmth of her arousal.

A low, breathy moan tumbled from her lips, and she tossed her head back, the click of the camera fading from her mind as erotic pleasure took over. Biting her lower lip, she stroked her aching, swollen flesh and clutched the pillow beneath her breasts as an explosive orgasm beckoned.

She heard a soft, explicit curse from somewhere behind her and gasped in startled surprise when the blanket was yanked away. Before she could react, Adrian was covering her from behind, gloriously naked, his skin searing hot, his body hard all over. Especially the erection nestling so insistently between her spread thighs.

She attempted to pull her hand away so that he could take over, but he wasn't having any of that. He grasped her wrist and kept her fingers in place. "No, don't stop," he ordered gruffly in her ear. "Guide me in."

She caressed the head of his cock with her fingers, lubricating him with her moisture before positioning his shaft at the core of her womanhood. His groan vibrated along her back as he slid in an excruciating inch. She arched her bottom against his hips, seeking more, just as he surged forward and filled her.

His slow, gyrating thrusts gradually gave way to deeper, heavier lunges that possessed and claimed her in an inherently primitive way. Reaching up, he entwined their fingers of the hand she'd curled into the pillow and slipped his other hand between her body and the mattress. He cupped her breast in his palm, squeezed and fondled the pliant mound, and lightly pinched her nipple between his fingers before skimming his hand lower, along her belly and down to her aching sex. His fingers joined with hers, adding to the hot, wet, slippery sensation along her clitoris, the dual, erotic stimulation causing her to whimper and rock frantically against his pistoning hips.

"Come for me," he rasped, and she felt his thighs

tighten along the backs of hers, felt his hot, damp, panting breaths rushing against the side of her neck, along with the arousing scrape of his unshaven jaw. "Oh, God, Chayse, *now*," he growled and pressed both of their fingers against her cleft, as deeply and rhythmically as his wild, untamed thrusts.

Her release crested right when his did, and they each rode out the exquisite pleasure of bodies meshing, hips pushing and straining, inner muscles clenching, and an incendiary heat that consumed them both.

Long moments later, Adrian rolled to his side, cradled her back against his chest, and whispered huskily in her ear, "Are you still grumpy?"

She laughed, unable to summon a grouchy reply, even a playful one, when she felt so sated. "Not in the least. What an amazing cure you've come up with," she murmured. "Ever thought of putting it on the market?"

"Can't," he said and dropped a warm, lingering kiss on her neck. "The remedy was designed solely for you, no one else, so I think you're stuck with me."

His meaning was clear, that he wanted to be stuck with her for a long time to come. She swallowed hard, battling more emotions, more insecurities, and feared that there was no cure or treatment for a troubling past that would always come between them.

Adrian's lungs burned, and the muscles in his thighs flexed and bunched as he sprinted up the steep path weaving alongside the hill behind the cabin. He'd been out jogging nonstop for nearly an hour now, letting the clean mountain air clear his mind and using the physical exercise to pump him up for what lay ahead between himself and Chayse—a confrontation where he would state his intentions and force her to finally acknowledge that there was more than just great sex between them.

The bit of solitude and mindless activity also gave him time to think, without Chayse distracting him with her luscious body and innate sensuality he couldn't seem to get enough of. Out here with nothing but nature's beauty to inspire him, he was able to finally come to terms with his own feelings for Chayse. That he was falling hard and fast for her.

It was as simple as that, and he wasn't going to fight something that felt so amazingly right to his heart and emotions. Though he had to admit that such a huge, life-altering revelation was both a scary and exhilarating prospect, like the first time he'd gone sky-diving and realized how much he loved the rush he experienced as he'd jumped out of the plane and soared through the sky. That's what Chayse was to him—a source of adrenaline for his mind, heart, and soul. And he wanted to experience that exciting, pulse-pounding rush on a daily basis.

Unfortunately, he still had Chayse's resistance to deal with—those soul-deep insecurities she'd allowed him to glimpse this weekend and those painful vulnerabilities that kept her from letting anyone too close for fear that she'd end up all alone again.

He'd learned that Chayse was all woman on the outside, tough and sexy and determined, but internally she was still a little girl, aching for the love and approval she'd never gotten from her parents and searching for a place where she belonged. A place stable and safe and filled with unconditional acceptance. A place where she didn't have to worry about the people who she trusted and loved turning their backs on her when times got tough and she needed them the most.

Adrian wanted to be there for Chayse, always—as a friend, a partner, and a lover. And it wasn't a commitment he planned to take lightly. Now all he had to do was convince her just how sincere he was, that he wanted this short weekend fling to last a lifetime.

He shook his head at how ironic it was that *he* was now the persistent one.

He picked up his pace, eager to be with her again. He grinned like a fool, finally understanding what his brothers had found with each of their wives. He'd given both Eric and Steve a hard time when they'd taken the plunge and admitted they'd fallen in love, and all the while, he'd sworn that he had no desire to let another woman get to him on an emotional level ever again. His brothers had been emphatic that it was a matter of finding the right woman, and he distinctly remembered Eric making the comment that he'd better be careful because falling in over his head might just sneak up on him and bite him in the ass when he least expected it.

At the time, he'd scoffed at Eric's sappy analogy. Now Adrian was forced to admit that he *had* been bitten when he'd least expected it, big-time, and both of his brothers were going to have a field day when they discovered his downfall. But it was a small price to pay for all that he'd gained.

Adrian's heart pumped anxiously as he rounded the bend in the road and came in for the home stretch, until he noticed that Chayse's car was no longer parked next to his jeep.

His stomach twisted with dread as the truth kicked him in the chest. He was too late to tell Chayse how he felt about her, to convince her to take a chance on him. She was already gone.

Oh, Lord, what had she done?

Pressing her fingers to her trembling lips, Chayse stared at the photos from her weekend with Adrian, which were spread out on her coffee table in her living room. Nearly six hours had passed since she'd left the cabin while Adrian was out on a morning jog. She hadn't heard from him since, not that she expected him to make any effort to find her after the less-than-admirable way she'd snuck out on him.

Her abrupt departure, along with the quick, impersonal note she'd left in the kitchen thanking him for being a part of her calendar project, had no doubt been as effective as a slap in his face after the intimate weekend they'd shared. At the time, she'd convinced herself that she was saving them both an unpleasant confrontation, that a clean break was easier on both of them, but alone in her apartment with only her conscience as company, she was coming to acknowledge her leaving for the cowardly behavior it was.

Her throat tightened with another surge of tears, and she swallowed them back as she leaned forward and fanned out a pile of pictures of Adrian looking sexier and more gorgeous than a man had a right to. There were phenomenal shots of him chopping wood and more they'd taken during their hikes. The majority had been taken without a shirt, his chest and shoulders breathtakingly wide and strong and most definitely drool-worthy. She was proud of the shots, and what you could glimpse of his scars only served to make him appear more rugged, like a real outdoor man who lived as one with nature.

He was extremely photogenic, and there wasn't a bad picture in the bunch, which made the task of finding only four for the calendar project a daunting task—the end results of which she'd promised Adrian he could approve. Which meant she'd eventually have to contact him and see him again in person.

She pushed aside the professional shots and reached for the candid photos she'd taken of Adrian while he'd been sleeping and had gradually awakened. A smile touched her lips as she remembered the playful, flirtatious session. Now she had her own personal storybook in front of her, and there was no ignoring what she saw in Adrian's gaze, in his expression. There was adoration, sensual hunger, and a deeper emotion that made her feel weak in the knees. A blend of trust and caring she'd been so scared to believe in.

Then there were the pictures Adrian had taken of her that morning, which told an interesting tale of their own. At first, she'd been uncomfortable being the focus of his attention, but he'd coaxed her to open up, to trust him, and she had—physically and emotionally, she realized as she picked up one of the photos of her seducing the camera and Adrian.

Her heart pounded so hard her chest hurt. Despite every attempt she'd made to keep her emotions out of the equation of the weekend, she'd gone and let him inside her heart. Her own story was right there in her eyes for her to see—the way she felt about him, along with the fact that she'd given him a piece of herself that would forever be his. Not just her body or her heart but her soul, as well.

His words came back to her, so accurate and sincere. *I look into your eyes, and I see a little girl who's carried a wealth of emotional burdens for too many years now and a woman who is afraid to take chances on what most likely is a sure thing. I see a woman who hides behind her camera, even while she tries to uncover everyone else's secrets.*

Adrian knew her well. And she knew without a doubt that he'd taken the pictures of her this morning because he'd wanted her to see what *he* saw in her. It was all there, insecurities and fears, the gradual sensual blossoming he'd cajoled out of her, and even the deep caring she hadn't realized had found its way into her heart.

She felt something wet trickle down her cheek and wiped away a tear. Then another. She caught sight of a picture of Adrian, the one where he was lying on the blanket near the creek, bare-chested and chewing on a blade of grass. But it wasn't the sexy smile that drew her or even the come-hither look in his eyes that told Chayse how much he wanted her. No, it was the scar that started a few inches above the waistband of his shorts—an injury he'd been so self-conscious of, enough to keep refusing her dozens of attempts to get him to pose for her charity calendar.

She traced the line in the photograph, remembering vividly how that puckered skin had felt beneath her fingers, her lips. She thought of the way she'd confronted Adrian about those scars when she'd arrived at the cabin, how she'd made him face them, deal with them, and not let an old injury affect his decision to do the calendar project. Those scars were a part of who and what he was, she'd told him.

She laughed around another bout of tears and knew she ought to take her own advice to heart. Adrian's scars were on the outside, hers were on the inside, but the suffering and insecurity that came with those wounds were the same. And it was time she confronted her own scars and her past. Face the pain, deal with it, and not let it affect her decision to let Adrian into her life.

A brisk knock on the door startled her, and she stood, swiping at her damp eyes and cheeks as she headed toward the entryway. She looked into the peephole and saw Adrian standing on the other side with a fierce expression on his face. He looked really pissed off, and she wondered at the wisdom of letting him inside. Maybe it was better if they had this conversation in the morning, after he'd cooled off a bit.

He banged on the door, rattling the wood and the chain securing the door. "Open up, Chayse," he ordered in an uncompromising tone. "Or else your neighbors are going to hear a very personal conversation out here in the hallway."

Knowing he was a man as good as his word and not wanting her neighbors to be privy to her personal life, she unlocked the door and opened it for him. He stormed into her apartment, his entire body fairly crackling with energy and a fury she knew he had every right to feel after the way she'd bolted on him this morning. His hair was tousled around his head, he hadn't shaved since the day before, and he looked not only exhausted but dark and dangerous, as well.

But she didn't fear him. Not at all. That he'd made the effort to figure out where she lived was a very positive thing, in her estimation. If he didn't care, he wouldn't be here. And she knew that wasn't the case with Adrian. If anything, he cared too much, and she was lucky to have found a man like him.

She exhaled a deep breath and asked very calmly, "How did you find out where I lived?"

He spun around and jammed his hands on his jean-clad hips. He glared at her, which did nothing to conceal the hurt she detected in his eyes, along with a brighter determination. "It wasn't easy. First, I had to hunt down Mia, who ought to wear a tracking device because I was one step behind her most of the afternoon. Once I found her, I demanded your address, and seeing that she owed me one for giving you the directions to the cabin, she cracked."

Chayse bit her bottom lip to keep from laughing, certain that Adrian wouldn't appreciate her finding humor at his expense. At least not at the moment, while he was so angry and hurt.

An awkward silence descended between them as he continued to glare at her, and she waved a hand toward the photographs on the coffee table. "Umm, since you're here, you can take a look at the pictures I took, and we can decide which ones you'd like to go into the calendar."

"At the moment, I don't give a damn about those pictures!" He stalked toward her, blue fire blazing in his eyes. "That's not why I'm here."

For every purposeful step he took forward, she took one back, until her bottom hit the edge of the small kitchen table that adjoined the living room. He closed the distance between them, and there was no mistaking the erection straining against the fly of his jeans and pressing against her mound.

She marveled at the fact that though he was definitely angry, he clearly still wanted her.

His gaze held hers as he tugged on the snap of her pants and ripped open the front placket. A frisson of excitement shot through her, making her feel alive and heady with anticipation, something only this man had the ability to trigger within her.

She knew what was going to happen, knew he was going to possess her in the most elemental way possible. Stake his claim on her. Brand her as his. An aggressive, wild mating that would bend her to his will and allow him to release the fury and anger swirling inside him in a purely sexual way. It was Adrian's way. Just like the first time he'd taken her so fiercely at the cabin, when she'd provoked him beyond his restraint.

He dragged her pants and underwear down her

legs and yanked them off, then quickly unbuckled his belt, unzipped his jeans, and freed his shaft. He lifted her so she was sitting on the edge of the table, and with his hands pressed against her knees, he widened her thighs and fit himself in between. She was already wet and aroused, and his erection slid along her slick flesh, the head of his cock burrowing into her weeping sex.

She braced her hands behind her on the table and shuddered, wanting this, but decided she ought to put up at least a token protest. "Adrian … what are you doing?"

A muscle in his cheek ticked. "Since you only seem to understand the way my body talks to you, I'm going to let it do the talking for me." He grabbed her ass and jerked her to the edge of the table the same time he flexed his hips and thrust into her, making her gasp at the depth in which he'd plowed.

He rolled his hips, grinding himself against her sex. "Do you know what my body is saying right now?" he demanded gruffly.

She shook her head, moaning as he slowly withdrew and quivering as he filled her again. "No."

"It's telling you that I want to be with you," he said, the tight edge in his voice softening as he pulled back and surged in again. "That I'm not going to ignore what's between us and I'm not going to let you walk away, either." Out … and back in again in a slow, languid stroke that made her melt around him. "I need you in my life, and you sure as hell need me in yours."

Her heart rejoiced, and she slanted him an assessing glance that gave nothing of her own emotions away just yet. "That's a little arrogant, don't you think?"

Watching her expression, he withdrew, and she whimpered at the loss, then gasped sharply when he returned, burying himself to the hilt. "I'm inside your body, sweetheart. As deep as I can get. I can feel your heartbeat. I can see the emotion in your eyes. I have every right to be arrogant. And demanding."

"Yes, you do," she agreed solemnly.

And then another revelation struck her. Adrian was all about taking risks, in everything he did—in his extreme sports, when making love, and even when it came to wearing his heart on his sleeve. As for her, she'd always played it safe, but not anymore. Not if she intended to meet this man halfway in all things. And that included trusting him with her heart and emotions. Right here and now.

With him full and heavy and throbbing inside her, she slid her hands into his thick, silky hair and nipped his chin, pressed a soft, open-mouthed kiss to his lips, then looked so deeply into his eyes she thought she'd drown in the unabashed emotion she saw shining there. The adoration. The hope and need that reflected her own.

She smiled and framed his face in her hands, and without any hesitation, she said, "Adrian Wilde, I'm crazy about you, and I want to be with you, too."

With a grateful moan, he captured her mouth with his, kissing her as deeply and fiercely as he plunged into her body. So much passion. Earthy and sensual and irresistible.

The ending came fast for the both of them, and when his climax rolled through him, she took his harsh groans into her mouth and gave back her own sweet sounds of release.

Amazingly enough, after that physically draining session, Adrian seemed to have enough strength to carry her to her bedroom, so she hung on for the ride and gave him directions down the hall. He set her gently on the bed and stretched out beside her, and she knew they still had a few things to discuss. But this time, she was ready to face the past and hopefully secure her future.

"Why did you leave the cabin today without waiting for me to return from my run?" he asked as he stroked his fingers along her arm. There was no censure in his tone, no more anger, just the need to understand.

She swallowed hard, and gave him an honest answer. "I was scared … mostly of what you make me feel, and my first instinct was to run from my emotions."

"What I make you feel is supposed to be a good thing, sweetheart," he murmured gently.

She stared up at him, feeling like the luckiest girl

on Planet Earth to have somehow earned this man's patience and understanding. "I know that now, but at the time, I wasn't ready to face my feelings or trust in them."

"Are you ready now?"

She nodded and whispered, "Yes."

He lifted a curious brow, obviously wanting more answers, which he fully deserved. "What changed your mind?"

"It was those pictures you took of me this morning. I saw myself through your eyes, just as you'd intended. All my emotions were right there in front of me, and there was no denying how hard and fast I'd fallen for you." She reached out and touched his unshaven jaw, loving the rough, arousing texture against her fingertips. "I don't want to keep living through the pictures I take of other people. I want to make my own storybook of memories, real ones, and I don't want be alone anymore, Adrian. I want to take a chance on a sure thing. I want to take a chance on you."

"Oh, yeah, I like the sound of that." He grinned, looking like the rogue of her dreams and the man who'd stolen her heart. "But taking a chance on me means being part of my big, crazy family. Think you can handle that?"

Her heart pounded crazily in her chest, the gift he was offering more than she'd ever believed possible. "Oh, Adrian, I would *love* to be a part of your family.

Do you think they can handle me snapping pictures of them when they least expect it?"

He chuckled, the sound reverberating with warmth and a bit of wickedness. "They'll get used to it."

She sighed blissfully, a huge smile on her face. "With each of us bearing our own scars, we're quite a pair, aren't we?"

"We're a perfect pair." He ran the tip of his finger down the slope of her nose, then he grew serious. "I know this has all happened so quickly, but I promise we'll work this relationship thing out, take whatever time you need to adjust to having me in your life."

"I don't need any more time, Adrian." Now that he was hers, there was no room left in her heart for uncertainties. She was risking it all. "I chased you for four months, and you've just given me the best weekend of my entire life. I want *you*, and nothing is going to change that."

"You're perfect, Chayse," he murmured, tracing a finger along her cheek. "Perfect for *me*."

She forced back the lump of emotion rising in her throat, his words chasing away every last bit of Chayse's insecurities, leaving her heart wide open for this incredible man to fill up with everything he had to give and offer.

Giddy with happiness, she wrapped her arms around his neck and pulled him on top of her, absorbing his declaration and wanting to preserve this precious moment forever, like a rare photograph in her mind. It was a wonderful beginning to her personal storybook of mental snapshots, and she was confident that her private album would only grow to reflect the best years of her life with The Wilde One.

Read on for an excerpt from the next book in the WILDE series, TOO WILDE TO TAME, featuring Cameron Sinclair and Mia Wilde!

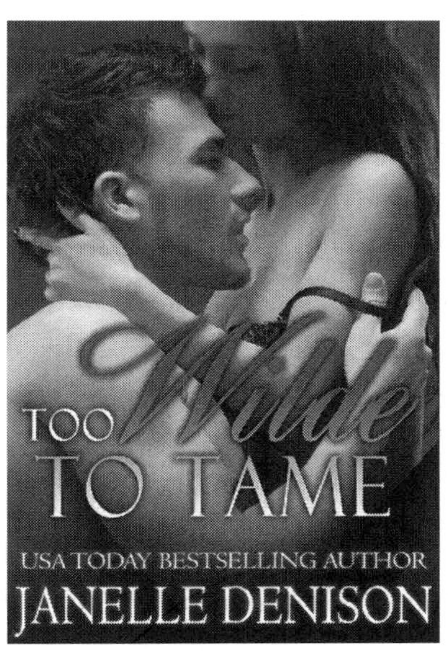

Chapter One

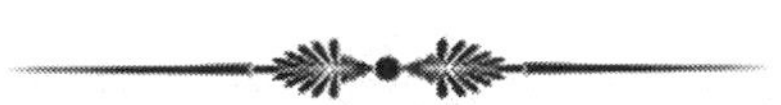

Cameron Sinclair took a long, satisfying pull on his ice cold bottle of beer as he surveyed the newest hot spot to open in downtown Chicago. The Electric Blue was definitely *the* happening place, and Cam could easily see why. It wasn't your normal laid-back bar atmosphere, but rather the place combined the frenzied excitement of a nightclub with all the shocking yet riveting antics worthy of a roadhouse saloon—where customers were having Screaming Orgasms, demanding Blow Jobs, and enjoying Slippery Nipples. The drinks, that is, he thought in amusement.

The place certainly didn't lack for entertainment. And as a people-watcher by profession, Cam was definitely stimulated and intrigued by the ambiance, the customers, and the decor. A huge oak bar with shiny brass trim covered the length of one long wall, where three bartenders were filling the constant barrage of drink orders while juggling bottles of liquor in the air and grooving to the beat of the rock and roll music the DJ was playing.

Cameron was sitting on a barstool up on a higher level across the room, which overlooked the main bar area and afforded him, and his good friend Rick, the best view in the house. In front of where they were sitting extended a thick, sturdy, two foot wide platform with floor to ceiling brass poles on either end, which, according to Rick, the waiters and waitresses used as their own personal dance floor to rile up the crowd whenever one of the bartenders rang a loud, obnoxious cow bell every half hour.

The dance floor, also on the same higher level, was fully packed with gyrating bodies and scantily clad women, and a banner across the back wall proclaimed tonight "Wet T-Shirt Night". That was the main reason why Rick had coaxed him into joining him for a beer at The Electric Blue, because his friend believed Cameron was spending way too much time at work, and not enough time having fun and enjoying the opposite sex.

Okay, so it had been a while since he'd been out with a woman on a casual, no-strings basis. Longer still since he'd been in a committed relationship. His heavy caseload and erratic hours as a P.I. was mainly responsible for his lack of female companionship, and after the busy week he'd had at work, Cameron decided that what he needed was exactly what Rick had suggested. A fun, entertaining evening—and The Electric Blue promised to deliver all that, and more.

Cameron took another drink of his beer, feeling his body unwind and his mind open up to the possibilities of what the night might hold.

"Well, well, well," a familiar, sultry female voice drawled from behind him, followed by the sensual trail of fingertips along his shoulders as she came to stand in front of him. "What's a nice, straight-laced guy like you doing in a place like this?"

Cam recognized the soft taunting voice before he saw the face that went with it, and every muscle in his body grew taut with immediate awareness.

Mia Wilde—an infuriatingly smart-mouthed woman who had the ability to frustrate the hell out of him with her bold and brash ways, as well as tempt him beyond reason with her innate sensuality.

Despite all the reasons why this certain female was

all wrong for him, and there were many, *she* was the main reason why no other woman had appealed to him in a very long time.

Maintaining a bland expression, he slowly, leisurely glanced up the length of her figure, taking in her sexy bare legs and smooth, supple looking thighs that never failed to make him entertain sinful, erotic thoughts. Her curvaceous hip was cocked sassily to the side, and she was wearing a short leopard print mini-skirt that was barely street legal, along with a tight black top with "*Too Wild To Tame*" emblazoned in sparkling rhinestones across her ample chest.

He almost laughed out loud. The flashy slogan was very appropriate, not because of the similarity to Mia's last name but because this particular woman was unpredictable, headstrong, and aggressive enough to make any sane man dismiss the notion of ever trying to subdue that assertive nature of hers.

Him included. He liked his women modest, manageable, and undemanding. And Mia was anything but those things. She was a woman who didn't know the meaning of demure and refused to conform to anyone's rules but her own. She liked being in control and was used to getting her way. Especially when it came to men. One come hither smile, one crook of her finger, and the male gender turned into whipped little puppies who were eager to please while hoping for more of her attention.

And Cam knew, beyond that sexy, confident facade Mia presented in front of him, deep inside it irked the hell out of her that he was immune to her sensual charms. Or at least that's what he'd spent the past two years pretending. No way would he ever give her the satisfaction, or the leverage, of knowing she affected him on a sexual level—and that only made her all the more determined to prove that he *did* have the hots for her.

It was an ongoing battle between them, a push-pull kind of magnetism that always generated a whole lot of heat and lust whenever their paths happen to cross. Which was much too often lately for his peace of mind and sanity.

Finally, his lazy gaze reached her face, and he had to admit it was one of great beauty. Silky, tousled shoulder-length black hair framed her exquisite features and added to her exotic look. Her complexion was smooth and creamy, and she possessed the kind of lush, Angelina Jolie mouth that inspired all kinds of provocative, X-rated fantasies. Those full lips were painted a soft, shimmering peach hue, and when he reached her gaze, her smoky silver eyes glimmered impudently, prompting him to remember the question she'd just asked, along with the fact that she'd pretty much accused him of being stuffy and boring.

No big surprise there.

He leaned back in his seat and regarded her with mild interest. "So what, exactly, do you consider this place?"

"Hip. Fun. Trendy." She took a sip of the drink she held in her hand, which looked like a frothy Piña Colada, then her glossy lips curled up in one of those slow, cheeky smiles of hers.

"You know, the exact opposite of your uptight personality," she said as she glided a finger along the collar of his knit shirt and down the buttoned v-neck.

Beside him, Rick chuckled at her reply, and Cam shot his friend a withering glare. "Don't encourage her," he muttered.

As soon as Cameron addressed his friend, Mia turned her gaze toward Rick, curiosity lighting up her eyes. "Who's your friend, Sugar?"

Rick, as much of a bachelor as Cameron was, looked eager to make Mia's acquaintance. Too eager, Cam thought in annoyance, but made the introduction anyway. "This is Mia Wilde. Mia, this is a friend of mine, Rick."

Rick's brows rose in surprise. "Any relation to your business partner?" he asked Cameron, obviously recognizing her last name.

"Yes, I'm Steve Wilde's cousin," she said before Cameron had the chance to explain. Completely ignoring Cam, she extended her slender hand toward Rick, who didn't refuse the opportunity to touch her. "It's a pleasure to meet you."

She poured on the flirtatious charm, and that easily she ensnared herself yet another besotted admirer. Rick grinned at her, completely captivated. "Ummm, likewise."

Their handshake lingered longer than necessary, and despite Cam's resolve to keep his involvement with Mia on a casual, amicable level because of his business partnership with her cousin Steve, he felt the unfamiliar stirring of envy rising to the surface. And that wasn't a good sign, considering he didn't give a damn who Mia set her sights on.

Or so he sternly reminded himself.

His fingers tightened around his bottle of beer. "So, who are you here with?" he asked abruptly, recognizing his own ploy to interrupt the warm, cozy moment between Mia and Rick.

"I came with my roommate Gina and her new boyfriend Ray, and another friend, Carrie." She pointed to a table across the way where her three friends were sitting, then tipped her head toward Cameron and cast him a sly, knowing look. "Were you wondering if I came here with a date?"

"Does it look like I care?" He tipped his beer to his lips and took a long drink.

She leaned in close, her lashes falling half-mast over her beguiling gray eyes. "Oh, you care, Sugar," she said in a low, husky tone that was as intimate as a caress. "You don't want to, but you do."

He watched her lips move as she spoke and inhaled the sweet, fruity scent of her drink on her breath. His gut clenched with a smoldering heat and desire, giving too much credence to her words.

With effort, he managed a cool, indifferent response. "Don't flatter yourself, sweetheart."

Mocking laughter lit up her gaze. "And you just keep trying to fool yourself into believing otherwise." Straightening, she set her glass on the table and redirected her attention back to Rick. "So, would you like to dance?"

Rick replied with an enthusiastic "Sure," at the same time Cameron said, "We're not here to dance."

Too late, he realized just how ridiculous he sounded—especially since they were in a bar with a DJ and dance floor. But dammit, he didn't want her dancing with Rick.

He swore beneath his breath.

"Obviously *you're* not here to have a good time, but Rick *is*," Mia said, taking the opportunity to point out just how stuffy she thought Cameron really was. She held out her hand toward his friend and gave him a dazzling smile no red-blooded man could resist. "I'm looking for a dance partner. You interested?"

Rick jumped up and grabbed Mia's hand, nearly knocking over his barstool in his haste to accept her offer. "I'm not about to refuse a lady."

Cameron snorted at the term *lady*, but his attempt at sarcasm was lost in the wake of their departure. Annoyed at Mia's calculated attempt to provoke him, which had worked too well, he watched as the two of them made their way through the throng of people in the bar and up to the crowded dance floor.

The loud, upbeat music combined with the pulsing colored lights flashing above the dance stage encouraged a person to shed inhibitions and move to the suggestive rhythm—and Mia didn't hesitate to do exactly that. Despite all the other women bumping and grinding up on the stage in tight, skimpy outfits, his gaze never strayed from Mia—and every once in a while he caught her glancing his way as well, as if to make certain he was watching her have a good time with his friend.

Every one of her movements were damn sexy and arousing, and he couldn't help but notice that he wasn't the only guy in the place that was drawn to her. She was naturally sensual, her body loose and unrestrained as she rolled and swayed her hips in time to the music. Then she turned, raised her hands above her head in sheer abandonment, and shimmied her curvaceous backside against the front of Rick's jeans. The other man made a grab for Mia's hips to pull her closer, and she laughed and easily slipped away in a lithe move that was as playful as it was teasing.

Cam clenched his jaw, along with his fist, shocked by the uncharacteristic and too possessive urge he had to plant his knuckles against Rick's jaw for being way too intimate with Mia—even if *she'd* been the one to encourage his friend to be a little touchy-feely in her attempt to incite some kind of reaction out of Cam.

Typical Mia. She never missed an opportunity to taunt, tease, and provoke him in her never ending quest to see just how far she could push him before he finally snapped and gave into the heat and attraction simmering between them.

It wasn't going to happen, he vowed. He'd spent the past two years resisting her, and no way would she ever find out just how much she aroused him, and just how badly he wanted her. Doing so would undoubtedly be his biggest downfall, and her greatest triumph.

***Find out what happens between Cam and Mia in** TOO WILDE TO TAME!*

Other Books Available in the "WILDE" Series

THE WILDE ONE

WILDE THING

THE WILDE SIDE

TOO WILDE TO TAME

BORN TO BE WILDE

WILDE FOR HIM

About the Author

Janelle Denison is a *USA Today* Bestselling author of over fifty contemporary romance novels. She is a two time recipient of the National Reader's Choice Award, and has also been nominated for the prestigious RITA award. Janelle is a California native who now calls Oregon home. She resides in the Portland area with her husband and daughters, and can't imagine a more beautiful place to live. When not writing, she can be found exploring the great Northwest, from the gorgeous beaches to the amazing waterfalls and lush mountains. To learn more about Janelle and her upcoming releases, you can visit her website at: www.janelledenison.com.

Other places to find Janelle on the internet:
www.facebook.com/janelledenisonfanpage
www.twitter.com/janelledenison

Made in the USA
Lexington, KY
19 May 2016